Praise

"50 Give or Take is the itsy bitsy teenie weenie yellow polka dot bikini of writing." Teri M Brown

"Thought-provoking petite prose." Theresa Milstein

"Tiny windows that sometimes are also tiny mirrors." Tim Canny

"I have finally found a good way to start my day: 50 words of creative prose, instead of 50 screams about the news." Joel Savishinsky

"Bite-sized stories that deliver substantial thought and massive inspiration." Melanie Faith

"A literary diet guaranteed to shed verbal flab." Ann S. Epstein

"It's a 50-50, win-win, first-thing-in-the-morning icebreaker." Linda Romanowski

"Like ants on a crawl, these stories carry 50 times their weight impacting your day with wit and wonder." Pasquale Trozzolo

"Sometimes what you leave out tells more of the story than your words can." Peter Snell

"50 ways to get to the heart of the matter." Joanne Nelson

"Choose your words carefully and 50 may be all you need." Mary Boone

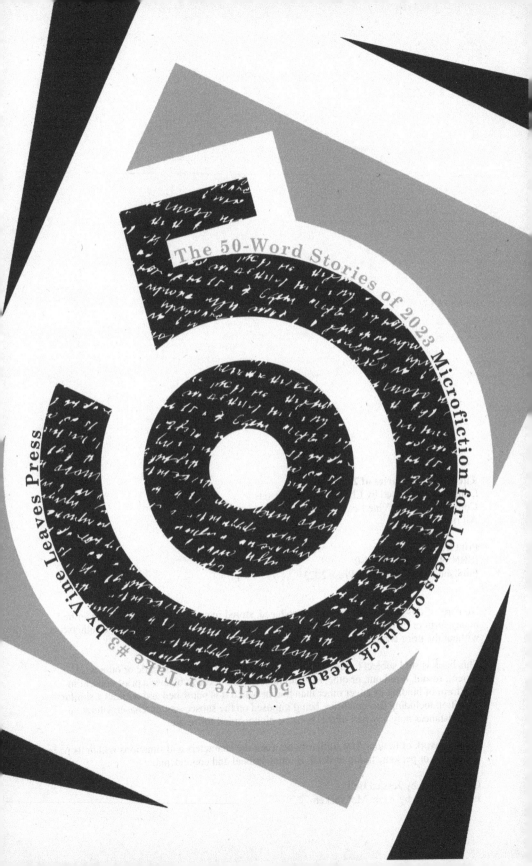

The 50-Word Stories of 2023

Microfiction for Lovers of Quick Reads

50 Give or Take #3

by Vine Leaves Press

The 50-Word Stories of 2023
Compiled and edited by Elaina Battista-Parsons

Print Edition
ISBN: 978-3-98832-036-0
Published by Vine Leaves Press 2023

Cover design by Jessica Bell
Interior design by Amie McCracken

Butterflies Die Too

As I cross the road, purple, blue, red flutters, unable to catch flight. I place her in my palm. Dying feathers tickle my skin. If only there was an emergency room I could take her to, a doctor I could call. I lay her down under a winter tree, her movements shallow. Still. Goodbye, my friend. Butterflies die too.

M.R. Mandell is a writer living in Los Angeles, CA, with her partner and her muse, a Golden Retriever named Chester Blue. *mrmandellpoet.com*

Trapped

Yesterday, a faint fluttering on mesh revealed a small gray bird trapped on the screen porch. In alternating bouts of fear and fatigue, it flashed feathers, unable to detect the open door three feet away. Only my looming shadow helped it flee from the corner into open air.

Jean Janicke is an economist and writer living in Washington, DC.

Never Mind

The day she lost her mind she wondered whether she had tucked it away somewhere, crammed high on the shelf with unused kitchen appliances. Or banished to the cupboard, a shadow memory to keep her old photos company. Until it returned, much later than expected, she simply became someone else.

Pierlot is an Australian author and playwright who enjoys exploring big ideas (when she's not growing avocados and hanging out with the resident echidna). *maurapierlot.com*

Tribute to an Exceptional Leader

An endless smile, sparkling eyes and calming voice. Modeling, she leads, and her team confidently blossoms. Fair, firm and consistent nurturing little minds, soothing skinned egos and guiding tiny hands into the future. She is a sage force leaving a positive impression and humanity is better because of her wisdom.

Deb Obermanns is an avid traveler, lover of storytelling, and international schoolteacher.

The New Boy

Seven schools in seven years. Victor's principal stopped him on the way to class.

"I'm just wondering, Victor," the principal said. "Why does your family move so much?"

"We don't," Victor said and moved on down the hall. That night, the boy entered through an open window, matches in hand.

Cathy Mellett's stories and memoirs have appeared in *The Michigan Quarterly*, *The Rumpus*, *The Southwest Review*, and elsewhere.

Elusive

Gulls wing through yellow, orange, and red—blending, moving, converging the light as they dive and call. The air, ripe with fish and salt and a dash of sand is cool against my skin in the fading light. I strain to capture the peace silently slipping below the horizon.

Teri M Brown, author of *Sunflowers Beneath the Snow*, connects readers to characters they'd love to invite to lunch. *terimbrown.com*

End of a Dry Season

The lovely, soothing water dreams were back. They had evaporated by the time Stella reached midlife. Now they were back, with water always bearing her up, even as it drowned others. Unintentionally, Julie pinpointed with one question why they had returned. "So, how are you sleeping since Frank left?"

Deborah Jones is a retired TV news writer/producer with a passion for wombats, red wine, and Oxford commas—not necessarily in that order.

The Gift of Tears

Again, he crossed the busy Wall Street sidewalk. Again, he thought of the child; gone before he knew it had even existed. Again, his tears fell on leather as he slid into the back of the black sedan. This time was different though. This time he never stopped crying.

Tim is a writer in the dust of middle age specializing in children's stories characterized by a misguided sense of whimsy. *@tcanny*

Endless Sleep

Lying peacefully. Her eyes are closed, but her hair is all wrong. Shrouded by cream silk. I hold her motionless hands and kiss her cold soft cheek. "Wake up Mum," I whisper, but her sleep is too deep, it's the sleep you never wake up from.

Alison Davidson is a Brit living in New Jersey with a passion for dogs, hiking, and now writing!

Silence

"I hate the blue with the yellow," he spat with pent-up venom. The dissipating energy of the shock hisses between them, a sprung Jack-in-the-Box, bouncing slower and slower. "We'll talk about it tomorrow," she manages. His sullen nod creates a chasm of silence. She's certain he'll be gone by then.

Keren Dibben-Wyatt is a chronically-ill Christian contemplative, author, and artist living in the UK. *kerendibbenswyatt.com*

Ritual Ambivalence

Occasionally, we'd drive to the coast. His Peugeot 205 trundled along to Chris de Burgh and found the familiar village lined with sleepy houses and shops with sun-bleached notices in windows. He brings me because I love the sea. But it's not the Med.

Teresa Renton lives in North Yorkshire, UK where she writes fiction and poetry and creates further stories through her interest in photography. *vocal.media/authors/teresa-renton*

Oh

I'm washing dishes when my favorite auntie comes up behind me. "Happy sixteenth!" she says, squeezing my shoulders, giving them a little massage with her thumbs. I love when she does that. Then she slides her hands down my back. This is new. And around my waist. Oh. Oh!

Christine Ries loves capturing a moment, idea, story, or image.

The Bandit

He slinks stealthily, silent, keeping hidden in the shadows of the fading sunlight. Climbs a pine tree searching for suet left for the birds, but just as sweet to his tooth. Partway up, he spots a dreaded human! The raccoon reconsiders the situation—right to privacy—it opts for another tree.

Pete Obermanns is a retired Navy helicopter pilot who lives in Germany, and a big fan of sci-fi and SpaceX.

Underground Cathedral

His robe the bib of overalls, his tippet battery cable sashed to the taper of his miter; cap against a black sky. Pick axe scepter swinging from his kneeling space against a bituminous altar, prayerfully working in the sanctity of the ordinary.

Jack Albert is a poet of sorts, lover of history, and writer of small things.

Return to Tiffany

The nurses removed the silver charm bracelet you'd worn faithfully these many years. The links jingled as it fell on my outstretched trembling palm. The bracelet, still warm. The top of the heart charm had worn down to a thin line. If not mended, it would soon fade away too.

A special education teacher by day, Theresa Milstein writes middle grade, YA, and dabbles in poetry. *theresamilstein.blogspot.com*

Fireball

Both early for the staff meeting, they picked out trucker names from an app using their first pet name and birth month. Puff Fireball and Socks Fireball. She had no idea they had the same birth month. For a full five seconds, she was in love.

Chara Campanella is an Emmy-nominated writer/producer whose work can be seen everywhere children have eyeballs. *yawpshop.com*

Buzz

In bed one night, I leaned over to put my iPad and lap desk on the side table and accidentally turned on my vibrator. Buzzzzzzzzzzzzzz. Stay calm. I put down the iPad and desk and picked up Big Blue. He's silenced. I look cautiously across the bed. Husband didn't stir.

Honey Rand has been writing since she could hold a pencil--now she doesn't need to. *honeyrand.com*

Bottomless

She desperately tries to fill the holes. But they are bottomless pits. They are walls lined with all of her failures, fears, frustrations, unhappiness, and, of course, pain. No one understands. No matter how hard she attempts to explain. So she eats a second portion and then a third.

Phil loves doing Wordle, playing Pickleball, and writing short fiction, of which, many have made it into magazines.

Mothers Don't Always Know

Don't swallow your gum. Your face will stick like that. You'll ruin your eyes sitting so close to the TV. Always wear clean underwear. Mother's advice was meant to keep me safe. Who would have thought I'd be reading a good book when I learned of the cancer?

Teri M Brown, author of *Sunflowers Beneath the Snow*, connects readers to characters they'd love to invite to lunch. *terimbrown.com*

It's Greek to Me

"I shall slay him for besmirching your honor!" Syphilis raised his sword. His sister, Chlamydia, hugged his legs. "No, Brother! I love Herpes, he is brave and loyal!" Just then, their mother, Gonorrhea entered the room. "Stop this childish nonsense! We dine with Hepatitis and his wife Papilloma this evening."

Michael Yoder is a published writer living in Victoria BC, Canada whose work includes short stories and novellas.

Rome

Black-veiled women hunched in pews on polished marble floors. Narrow lanes with meat on spits. Slate-cold air in skull-lined catacombs. Voices of women in the eternal city, where life and death coexist, cherishing il Papa but ignoring him on birth control, no less spiritual for it.

Anna Marie Laforest is a poet and cozy mystery novelist who can eat chocolate and listen to opera at the same time. *annamarielaforest.wixsite.com*

Good Thinking

A frigid summer night on arid scrubland. Camels snorting huddle alongside the yurt sheltering from the winds. Pulsating stars throughout an inky sky blanket the vastness. A swift dash to the latrine becomes disorienting. Geographical reference; the white stupas invisible. Pause, think, horizon ... satellites orbit west to east. Mongolia!

Deb Obermanns is an avid traveler, lover of storytelling, and international schoolteacher.

Closed System

There is no new water. We have now all the water that's ever been. Dried tears of displaced first peoples fall as rain on my lawn. The water itself is displaced—leaving behind parched expanses to envy the killing floods elsewhere. Is it too late to send the water home?

Deborah Jones is a retired TV news producer and late-blooming writer of fiction.

He Always Wanted Children

On his fiftieth birthday, Sam regretted not having any children. After dating Henrietta a few weeks he suggested they marry. She agreed with the proviso they move to her home in the suburbs. "I have two goats," she informed him. "Well, I always wanted kids," he responded.

Zvi A. Sesling, Brookline, MA Poet Laureate, has published poems and flash/micro fiction and four volumes and three chapbooks of poetry.

False Flag

They stand beside their desks, reciting words they know by heart but don't yet genuinely understand. Suddenly, the door swings open. Their pledge to a country that refuses to protect them is left unfinished as chaos erupts. Their hands over their hearts offer no shield from the spray of bullets.

Elizabeth Barton rearranges words for fun and profit while living in Chicago with her husband, two cats, and ample self-doubt. *lizardesque.wordpress.com*

Merit of Rain

He dislikes storms. They spoil fun, inconveniencing everything but one. Against the gusty winds, he puts the last shovelful of dirt, covering up the hole. Tossing the bloodstained shovel to ground, he smiles contentedly as the rain sheets down, washing off all the traces.

Ling Chiehyun, bewitched by the charm of stories, dreams to work in this world of unlimited imagination.

Diner Eggs

Coffee to Dad's right. Salt, pepper on left. Mama's tea: cream, sugar swirling, a sexy rumba. Devouring jelly packets from the acrylic cubby, meant for buttered toast. Golden eggs, crumbly bacon, crunchy home fries, crisped rye: NJ diners! That booth became home. Waitress clears food campsite. OJ glass frowns. Breakfast disappears.

Jade Visone writes with soul-filled honesty about the struggles and magic of mothering, love, life, dandelions, and stars. *@mrsvisoney*

Investments

I prided myself on the fact that I was as far away from being a material girl as one could be. I know capitalism is the root of most evil. But at sixty-four I want and think I need good socks and comfortable shoes, good sheets and a comfortable mattress.

Connie Biewald teaches and writes in Cambridge, MA and Matènwa, Haiti. *conniebiewald.com*

Rattle

I heard a rattle. More like the sound of sizzling oil than a Maraca or a baby's toy. I stood up and listened. The sound came from a boulder to my left. A rattlesnake. I inched right, walking stick in hand, then loudly stomped down the mountain. Beware critters.

Mary Janicke is a gardener and writer living in Houston, Texas.

Splintered

The shard of twenty-plus-year-old paint slid under her nail and into the quick. "Damn it!" Tears streamed in response to her timidity for staying decades too long. Better life beckoned if she had the nerve to leave and explore. Maybe. She returned to scraping the deck and just passing time.

Shauna Lee Sanford McCarty is a retired educator who enjoys wordplay of all kinds.

The Sleep Doctor

The man entered her office. "I understand you give your clients what they need, enabling them to sleep better?" Her new client asked. "That's a simplistic way of putting it but yes, that's true," the doctor answered. "Good," he whispered, tightening a scarf around her neck with a deadly grip.

Gypsie-Ami Offenbacher-Ferris is a poet and author living in Southport, NC. *gypsieswritingmusingsquotesgripes.wordpress.com*

Funny?

The eraser sits on his desk. "Hey," I say. "You've got a rubber ducky rubber." He replies, "I've got a rubber rubber ducky rubber." We laugh. Later, in the staff room, nobody sees the humor. I hope my seven-year-old friend fared better with his peers.

Natalie Bock is an ex-military, non-conformist theologian in training who regularly scribbles poetry and snippets of stories on any paper she can salvage from her handbag.

Sub Miss/Sub Sunk

A naval exercise, with a submarine. Tracking, attacking. Suddenly, no contact. Calls on underwater loudspeakers—unanswered. Captains of surface ships nervously consult on secure radio—should we alert the Pentagon? Eventually, the sub contacts on radio—skipper was bored and left to go feed his crew lunch.

Pete Obermanns is a retired Navy helicopter pilot who lives in Germany, and a big fan of sci-fi and SpaceX.

Foam

Raspberries on a branch, red as drops of blood, Walk your feet on the sand, let them leave a mark that time will erase. You are from the foam, like a little mermaid, and you will pass into the foam, courage for others, you are like a leaf brought here.

Irina Tall (Novikova) is an artist, graphic artist, illustrator, writer who loves nature, hiking, and jerboas.

The Funeral Home

St. Joseph's Funeral Home replaced the candy factory overnight but retained the smell of burned chocolate and fresh plastic. St. Joseph's had many windows—plenty for passersby to peer in while the bereaved gazed out—and mesmerized children pulled their mothers' hands, begging to be buried in insurmountable sugar.

Remi Recchia, four-time Pushcart Prize nominee and author of *Quicksand/Stargazing* is a trans poet and essayist from Kalamazoo, MI.

The White Rabbit

I was running. Why was I running? Raindrops hit the umbrella like gunshots aimed at my ears. A car screeched and honked in anger while an empty shop sang the latest hits. My shoes belched water at every step. The world was so loud, and I was late. For what?

Rebecca Ahn is a Korean-American writer from Seattle who loves all things literary. *@toastieghostie.writes*

Familiar

It's at the other end of this corridor. I can feel it. Waiting for the library to empty. Students are being ushered from the building. I hide in the recess, clasping the ancient book of spells. Heart pounding in anticipation of the power I have unleashed. That will be mine.

Rosie Cullen lives in Manchester, UK, and likes writing all kinds of little stuff but still loves her big novel *The Lucky Country* best. *mcullenauthor.wordpress.com*

Semper Deinceps

The ancient family motto "Always Forward" was bred into Laurent's DNA. He thought nothing of racing toward his destination, despite the raging storm and zero visibility. When the road dropped from under the Jag he realized the bridge was out, and why, maybe, he was the last of his line.

Tim is a writer in the dust of middle age specializing in children's stories characterized by a misguided sense of whimsy. Twitter *@tcanny*

Museum Trip

In the museum's gift shop that summer, I admired the calendar with photos of their garden sculptures. You took the display copy from the top of the pile. Seven-year-old me longed to shrink to nothing as you haggled for a bigger discount. You always did want something for nothing.

A special education teacher by day, Theresa Milstein writes middle grade, YA, and dabbles in poetry. *theresamilstein.com*

City Wheels

That the Red Cross cot frightened me, that my blood was too late, that he'd asked me to go along last night, that by some jealous grace I'd said no. In one hurtle his car jumped lanes, went up an embankment, and spit him out onto the Detroit grass.

Anna Marie Laforest is a poet and cozy mystery novelist who can eat chocolate and listen to opera at the same time. *annamarielaforest.wixsite.com*

Springtime

Most of all, it was springtime. We always knew, her saying, "listen to the sounds in the marsh." I pointing to the crocus peeping. Again, it is springtime, I know. Sounds in the marsh and crocus peeping. Most of all, I am missing her.

Jack Albert is a poet of sorts, lover of history, and writer of small things.

Loss of Seeing Eye

I buried Marshall under the maple tree. Come fall, the leaves will give off fireworks of color, a worthy tribute to his service. I sense him waiting to lead me home. I reach out to touch my phantom companion. Blind anew, life seems darker and my world that much smaller.

Nina Miller is a micro and flash fiction addict who's engaging in the novel act of writing a novel. *ninamillerwrites.com*

Coming and Going

The hospital reported the birth of baby Eric the day Eric Johnson fell off a scaffold at the new hospital they're building out by the Carnation Milk plant. A dowel in the pediatric wing foundation pierced his heart and exited his armpit. Folks couldn't pay their respects without snickering.

Tony Tinsley is an author and editor who divides his time between the Pacific Northwest and St. Louis-Southern Illinois areas in the United States.

Colonie Shopping Mall

My sister steals pennies from fountains to buy earrings at Claire's. Her bare feet wade in bubbling, shallow water. Squatting like a frog, she picks up hundreds of shiny coins. Where's my mother? All that matters is she doesn't get caught and that her earrings won't rust.

Sherri Levine is a poet living in Portland, Oregon and has been published in *50 Give or Take* print edition.

Central Park

Darkness had fallen across Central Park, and at the same moment that I looked out, the lights along its walkways and roads at once illuminated, glittering yellow and white, like stars fallen at my feet. The heavens seemed to have been suddenly turned upside down.

Edward Di Gangi writes with a passion for people, place, and discovery. *digangiauthor.com*

Vintage Varmints

Penny's sister, Mia, liked the latest things: pleated tees, Balkan boy bands, fennel gummies. Penny preferred old stuff: her one-speed Schwinn, Granny's cut-glass candy dish, Little Richard 45s. So it was no surprise when Mia named her dog-breeding business Hungarian Mudi Mart. And Penny named her pet adoption foundation Vintage Varmints.

At five feet give or take, Ann S. Epstein appreciates what is short, but is also a fan of long stories, long-stemmed roses, and long summer days. *asewovenwords.com*

In the Koi Pond

The brightly-colored koi swam lazily in the koi pond. The sun beat down as it usually does on cloudless days. A breeze barely stirred the surface of the koi pond. Then the famished ducks arrived. Then far fewer brightly-colored koi swam gently, lazily ...

David Sydney is a physician from Newtown, Pennsylvania.

Poker Face

Ben liked to say, "If you don't see the sucker at the table, it's you." But Ben did not play poker. After Ben was laid off, he met his friend Sara at a café. A window sign said Help Wanted. Ben repeated, "Help Wanted." Sara could see right through him.

Gary Campanella is a writer and editor who lives in Los Angeles, so there's that. *garycampanella.com*

Hope

The purposeful weed kept growing taller—two, four, six, eight feet, and more. Beneath her lofty leaves, her wildflower cousins sown with hope from the same seed packet, sport yellow and orange and pink and purple finery. I have faith in this magnificent weed. Soon she too will flower.

Mary Janicke lives, gardens, and writes in Houston, Texas.

Eda's Boarding House

A mother struggled to sustain her family, but Eda talented and tenacious persevered. Her Victorian home opened to students, sailors and singles she fried chicken, dished homegrown veggies and placed tall pitchers of sweet tea on communal tables. Forty years later, the veranda is still flowing with guests and Eda!

Deb Obermanns is an avid traveler, lover of storytelling, and international schoolteacher.

Evil People

Happiness folded the veil, and evil people came, tore up the flowers, leaving dried grass and threw something, it screamed a thousand times, shed tears and turned into a ghost. Trees grow up hugging the sky with branches, forgetting grief with flowers, wetting longing with leaves, having tasted the future.

Irina Tall (Novikova) writes a lot and invents fantastic creatures.

The Dance

Two men drape their biceps over her slender shoulders. One clutches her bum, the other has her in a chokehold—her face the shade of a prune, dress livid purple and orange. Something impossible among them—gravitational pull unmistakable. Will she break free and run before the dance ends?

Usually Dale Champlin writes poetry—today, she keeps the word count to fifty.
dalechamplin.com

Empathy

Standing at reception, radiating confidence and presence, long hair pony tailed, lithe dancer's legs browned by the Spanish sunshine. Alone, but not lonely. Between them, receptionist with abundant kindness, woman using Google Translate, the task is achieved. The refugee smiles her thanks and, with palpable relief, goes on her way.

Karen Jones can usually be found dreaming by the sea, seizing opportunities for adventures and loving the journey, dead ends and all.

Call a Plumber

"Damn clog," Jeremy said. "What's it gonna take?" He shoved down on the plunger, splashing foul water into his face. "You never said please," burbled a voice. "Puh-please?" A giant, scummy bubble rose to the surface and popped before water swirled down the drain. "Now, let's talk about your diet."

Matt Warnock is always thinking about stories and what-ifs, and it gets pretty noisy in his head sometimes.

Goodbye Summer

A wave washes away the sand castle. I look around for a sad child, but the beach is quiet. Only a few seagulls remain, darting about the sand, searching for the season's last crumbs of hot dog buns and pizza crust.

Lisa Marie Lopez loves the beach and has had short fiction published in *Blink-Ink* and *Potato Soup Journal.*

Get in There

The old woman's heart swells to see them, a new family, baby in her mother's arms, father kneeling next to the bed. He wants so much to touch them, but awe prevents him from reaching into the glow of God. "Go on," the midwife whispers. "Get in there."

Diane lives in the southwest US and has been doing nothing with her writing for a long time.

The Bruised Ones

While perusing the produce, she hears the fruit. A thick-skinned watermelon yells, "Choose me!" Overlooked apples mutter, "What's wrong with us?" and she shrugs sympathetically. The peaches are quiet. Yet she avoids them. Adjusting the sunglasses masking her swollen, blackened eye, she silently moves toward the frozen section.

Kate Bradley-Ferrall is a writer living in the Washington, DC area. *katebradleyferrall.com*

My Parents' Marriage

His dry wit kept her laughing seventy years. The only instance where that got her into trouble happened when she was nineteen and he was bringing her home to meet his parents. He got her laughing so hard as they climbed the porch steps that she drenched her own shoes.

Shoshauna Shy enjoys being with trees, books, cats, chocolate, and her husband, preferably all at the same time.

Gazing

He gazed in that special way nobody could resist. Or at least it had that effect on her. Dinner? Or at least a walk? Dinner might be out of the question, but it was a beautiful evening for a walk. She grabbed the leash.

A special education teacher by day, Theresa Milstein writes middle grade, YA, and dabbles in poetry. *theresamilstein.blogspot.com*

Time Capsule

In a stern voice Dad says, "Your room is a mess. You going to clean it?" "Yes." "When?" "Tonight." "Good!" He leaves my old room on his cane not remembering I've grown up, he's elderly and he made the mess. But experiencing the time capsule with him is a treasure.

Lisa Braxton is the author of the novel, *The Talking Drum,* for which she won an Independent Publisher (IPPY) Book Awards Gold Medal and Outstanding Literary Award from the National Association of Black Journalists. *lisabraxton.com*

On Rain & Rain Lamps

I'd feed the rain lamp, while my grandmother fed the cats. Neither of us interested in pretend play. Neither of us content to pretend. She'd lather mineral oils and read Greek mythology. I'd consume noodles and study Aphrodite. Bedtime was ten. All (f)oils capped. Performances ceased with the rain.

Jen Schneider is an educator who lives, works, and writes in small spaces throughout Pennsylvania.

Chi

She hurries out the side gate at sunrise while carefully setting her intentions. Her feet shuffling tiredly, begin to find their rhythm. She inhales confidence and exhales insecurity. She's connected to everyone and everything. Determined, she moves swiftly toward her future and all that infinite sunlight ahead of her.

Emily Kupinsky is a Weaver of Whimsy currently living her best life as an artist.

Alanna

Yes, a rare name: My mother wanted a boy, Dad a girl. His name's Alan; her's is Anna. They met in the middle, and I did, too, smack-dab, learned love is, lo-and-behold, a paradox, giving up, a heaven-bent compromise; the semicolon of life.

Leo Vanderpot has a note taped to the shade of his desk lamp: "… Anthony Powell said, 'Betjeman had a whim of iron.'"

Rova Farms

We stood among an expanse of gray granite headstones. Like pieces of glass tossed by the sea, each had been polished by seasons of swirling winter snows, sandy New Jersey soil blown by March winds, and the heat of the scorching summer sun on this bare unprotected hillside.

Edward Di Gangi writes with a passion for people, place and discovery. ***digangiauthor.com***

Paper or Plastic?

He'd endured the inane question for years, the option that wasn't an option. He didn't care, he never had. The path twisted and turned and ended up where it began. "Whatever works best for you," he said. Meltdown avoided. Balance restored. The tumor on his liver approved.

Jim Anderson lives in southeast Michigan and writes very short stories. *jimthewriter.net*

Gin Rummy Romance

The Queen of Spades swooned. The only card between her and that sexy Jack of Hearts was a Nine. Turning to the Queen of Diamonds, she whispered, "He's so hot." Just then the Queen of Hearts slid in between them. "Hands off, girls," she said. "That Jack's all mine!"

Rita Riebel Mitchell writes in South Jersey where she lives amongst the trees and wildlife with her husband. *ritariebelmitchell.com*

Wet Commute

For the fundraiser, Ted was doing his piece "Wet Commute," walking on the bottom of the Gaiman's pool, holding an umbrella. Bent as if into a breeze; raincoat swelling around him. My wife stood with our neighbors, applauding. She had a thing for artists who could hold their breath.

Chet Ensign writes and swims in northern New Jersey.

The Red Devil

"It'll turn your pee pink," the chemo nurse says as she sanitizes the port in my jugular vein. Then she pulls out a red needle that's bigger than her hand. I joke that she's gonna inject me with Kool-Aid. She laughs. I fake a smile and swallow a scream.

Jessica Brook Johnson is non-profit writer and cancer survivor who lives near Washington DC. *storiesfromtomorrow.com*

Exhortation

Their daily rituals easily passed for a relationship. From the outside, anyone would say that Frank and Stella had a good marriage. But without the coffee-making, newspaper-fetching, toast-buttering, and, later in the day, wine-drinking, and air-kissing, what was there? Rilke's ode to Apollo's torso urged, "You must change your life."

Deborah Jones is a retired TV news producer and late-blooming writer of fiction.

Ignorance Tax

Relocation, by choice or chance, creates situations that can be unfathomable. Prior life experience scarcely bridges the knowledge abyss. Challenges are often exciting yet costly. To soften the frustration of financial blunders simply laugh; you are being charged "Ignorance Tax." Shake your head, pay up and smile.

Deb Obermanns is an avid traveler, lover of storytelling, and international schoolteacher.

Creating Love

She knits colorful and lifelike birds. Golden ribbons are attached before they're released into the wild. After dark, she cycles to secret locations and hangs them high in the trees. They fly beneath the branches. The following morning, needles are clicking again. The next love bird is about to hatch.

John Holmes; a cyclist that writes and a writer that ... *johnholmeswriter.com*

Kill Then Eat

To eat something, first you need to kill it—the sprig of lettuce, the pumpkin seed, the piglet smarter than a dog, the fig, and the lobster. After the knife slices the tendon, the windpipe breaks free, wing bones crack and separate, fat sizzles. First, pray for the departed.

Usually Dale Champlin writes poetry, but today she keeps the word count to fifty.
dalechamplin.com

Eyes

Her dark almond-shaped eyes stare across the table searching for his, which she knows to be blue and are now averted. The din of the cafe buzzes around them. The coffee, poured only moments ago, waxes lukewarm. So have they. She rises and leaves, sure he doesn't even notice.

Susan R. Barclay is a writer and educator, who enjoys the simple things in life. *@susanrbarclay*

Imperial Problems

The Emperor had his problems. Revolts in the provinces. Pirates in the Mediterranean. Low grain supplies for distribution in Rome. Even the gladiatorial combats didn't lift his spirits. Could he be blamed for giving a thumbs down after each combat in the Colosseum?

David Sydney is a physician from Newtown, Pennsylvania.

Memories

Running from his past, Jack tripped over hopeful thoughts, mind hidden years ago. Rising, supported by refreshed memories, he met himself for the first time, returning from where he thought he wanted to be, all the while realizing if he had made that journey, he would never have known who he was.

Jack Albert is a poet, writer of little things, student of history.

The Brook

It had rained all night. Now the sun was out. She set out, sketchbook in hand, to capture the movement and sound of the brook. She heard the gurgle, roar, splash, and burble. Her watercolors brought the brook's swirl to life. The sounds remained an enigma.

Mary Janicke is a gardener, writer, and painter living in Houston, Texas.

Insomnia

The moon shines in and forbids sleep. Eyes open, her mind revs. At 4 a.m. she gives up, bakes cookies. Ambien tonight, she decides. After dreamless slumber she wakes refreshed and eats two ginger snaps for breakfast. Weeks later her picture surprises her in *50 Give or Take*: sleep writing.

Beth Manca is almost positive she wrote this while awake.

Coping Strategies

In-denial sister sends treats. Care-giver sister takes photos for WhatsApp. Mum drooping in a frayed armchair, vacant stare, chocolate box propped in a listless hand. Ever-supportive sister thanks, promises to pray for care-giver sister and mum. I peer at my phone, trying to see my mother. I write.

Judy Backhouse writes future fiction as an imaginative escape from research into technology and society (and pain). *judybackhouse.com*

Flirtini

"Make it a double," she said. Immediately drawn, I moved three stools down. That was my first mistake. "I'll have what she's having"—my second mistake. Then the big one, looking into those tumultuous eyes. Ten minutes of small talk, and I was in love—until her wife showed up.

Pasquale Trozzolo is a retired madman from Kansas. Still no tattoos, or MFA, he continues to complicate his life by living out as many retirement clichés as possible.

Burnout

She gave up coffee, right after she dumped booze and sour grapes—all her toxic friends. Now, every morning, she sips tepid tea from her favorite eggshell blue "Totally—the best mom—Ever" mug. A celebration of all the things she didn't lose, when she set her life on fire.

Jass Aujla plans perfect (fictional) murders in between her day-job meetings. *jassaujla.com*

Star Love

It was midnight. We lay side-by-side on the beach looking up at the sky. "There are seventy septillion stars in the universe, seven followed by twenty-three zeros. 10,000 stars for each grain of sand. That's a lot of stars," he said. And so it was that I fell in love.

Judith Shapiro secretly writes flash fiction when the novel she's writing looks the other way. *peaceineveryleaf.com*

Safe

Joe heard a gunshot followed by pounding on his cabin door. When he opened the door, a man holding his arm said "Somebody's trying to kill me. Let me in." A composed Joe said, "Don't worry, you're safe here." The stranger shot Joe. "You shouldn't have messed with my wife."

The author (Doug Hawley) has retired from a career in numbers and turned to writing.

Magic! Just Like That It's Gone

The therapist asked, *If I could wave a magic wand and you could have anything in the world, what would it be?* The woman said, *For me to be cancer free.* The therapist replied, *That's not realistic.* The woman shouted: *Neither is your magic wand!* Then realized shouting was very therapeutic.

Ellen Fox is an award-winning theater playwright, who has also written for radio, film, and television.

Star-Struck & Stuck on Stars

Growing up, evenings struck a similar routine. Heavenly noodles on Monday, Wednesday, and Friday. Rotating buffets of chili, tuna, and sardines in between. Campbell's Chicken & Stars on tap. The TV always on. *Hollywood Squares* on repeat. I'd sit by the window; my telescope pointed north. All of us star-struck.

Jen Schneider is an educator who lives, works, and writes in small spaces throughout Pennsylvania.

Gratitude

Over Dim Sum and tea, my husband expressed gratitude that during COVID's confinement, I didn't lounge around the pool, sipping Mimosas with my girlfriends complaining about his whining because of the lack of golf with his buddies. I said to him, "How could I? We don't have a swimming pool."

Rowena loves playing with words; a retired registered nurse living in Washington State.

Desperado

They picked him up crossing the freeway, maneuvering between the traffic, limbs extenuated against the blurry glow of headlights. Drones circled the area in a reel of white noise as sirens cut in and police cars blocked him. He dropped to the ground, a fetal lump in the middle lane.

Jenny writes and makes abstract ceramics.

Prickly Pair

Vague snipes arose between them, but this was the last straw. “Are you sure that’s a zucchini, not a cucumber?” “Shut up.” But at home, Stella sagged when she saw the cucumber in the grocery bag. Was it inevitable—becoming her mother looking for glasses that were on her face?

Deborah Jones wanted to be a tugboat captain but, with some regret, chose broadcast news writing instead.

The Scratch

Kaitlyn scratched that damn itch again. Temporary relief came. Others tried to calm it. All failed. Frustrated, she longed for someone to tame the persistent tickle. And then someone walked into her life. The woman’s long-nail scratch was euphoric, sent tingles down Kaitlyn’s spine, and the itch succumbed.

Philip Goldberg enjoys Wordle, playing pickleball, and writing short fiction, of which, many have made it into magazines.

Crack, Pop

Walking up the rutted drive, I felt the sun's heat through the soles of my shoes and the pebbles underfoot cracked with the sound of kernels of corn popping in a hot cast-iron skillet. The small shallow pond beside the road was filled with stagnant tepid water, snapping turtles, and water moccasins.

Edward Di Gangi writes with a passion for people, place, and discovery. *digangiauthor.com*

Telling Someone

Five a.m. at the photocopier, chatting with the math teacher, I said, "I fantasize about someone stabbing me in the stomach." "Huh," he said, surprised, "I dream of driving head on into oncoming headlights on my way home." And that's why, sometimes, telling someone doesn't make you feel better.

Kathryn Dettmer lives in Philadelphia with her husband, with whom she enjoys watching French crime dramas, their two children, and three cats.

Nero's Lyre

Officials of Rome's Fire Department announced today they have extended an invitation to Emperor Nero to provide the entertainment at their annual benefit dinner. Those in attendance will enjoy the main dish, which will be duck flambé served tableside. Tickets may be purchased at the firehouse for five denarii.

Roy Dorman enjoys reading and writing speculative fiction and poetry.

The Departure

A long time he sat by the window transfixed, watching his reflection dance like a devil on the panes. "I'm going," she said. And she left. He did not try to stop her. She did not look back. Stepping out into the cloudless day, her shadow did not follow her.

Richard Evanoff is active in literary circles in Tokyo, Japan as a writer and performer.

Goodbye Charlie

Holding my hand in front of his nose, his warm breath slowing to a relaxed slumber. I run my fingers through his thick, beautiful fur and the warmth I felt on my hand stops, his body stills. Face nuzzled into his, my tears flow as my heart shatters into tiny pieces.

Alison Davidson is a Brit living in New Jersey with a passion for dogs, hiking, and now writing!

Roots

Mum never could cope with my hair. Every day, steel tail scraping my head, she plaited inexpertly. As I got older, she couldn't help much with makeup, either. One day, a very old friend called. "She's the spit of Kofi." That's when I realized I was black. And Daddy wasn't.

Karen Jones can usually be found dreaming by the sea, seizing opportunities for adventures and loving the journey, dead ends and all.

Watched

Hidden by the bushes, he's watching her. Beside the picnic hut, I'm watching him. Gazing out to sea, she isn't aware of either of us. He hasn't noticed me watching him watching her either. Click. I shoot my photo and move on.

Natalie Bock is an ex-military, non-conformist theologian in training who regularly scribbles poetry and snippets of stories on any paper she can salvage from her handbag.

Second Date Guaranteed

Meet at a Mexican restaurant and order a hefty basket of fried tortilla chips with fresh salsa. While eating the chips, note if your companion offers to you the twisted, curled chips or only the flat ones. Curled chips create smiles, a second glance and another chance!

Deb Obermanns is an avid traveler, lover of storytelling, and international schoolteacher.

Killing Him Softly

The last needle thrust into this replica doll should put him to rest ... The old doc won't cure anyone anymore ... What? He's getting up! He seems younger ... stronger ... Wait! ... These needles ... They aren't mine ... They must be his ... The acupuncturist replaced them ... He knew my plan all along.

Paul Hertig enjoys dabbling with words and concepts in his free time. *apu.edu/clas/faculty/phertig*

On Tips of the Hat (& Heart)

I worked evenings at a local hat shop. Jolene on radio pre-sets. Mostly, I'd dream. Of a particular chap. His hat always tipped. Wore original bowlers on our first date. Decades later, our hats and hearts remained on deck. Hatboxes proof of love and (f)light in unexpected places (and headspaces).

Jen Schneider is an educator who lives, works, and writes in small spaces throughout Pennsylvania.

Harmless Ant

An ant chews on a piece of wood, a splinter in the wall. The homeowner sees and laughs. "A harmless ant," he says. The harmless ant leaves behind a scent invitation to a thousand more. They strip the base of the wall. Within a few years, the house is gone.

Robin Nemesszeghy enjoys weaving fantastical elements into realistic settings and exploring the complexities of the human mind. Medium *@robinnemesszeghy*

Mary Magdalene at the Empty Tomb

Your face was bloody, but I knew your voice when you cried out at the end. I've known it since you first said my name; I'd have followed it into the grave, but watched you laid in yours instead. So how is it you're here, speaking my name once more?

Morgan Want is a former journalist, who has been writing since her teens. She is currently as work on her first novel. Instagram *@wantmorgan*

Memorial Service

Ten years; the scar on the mountainside, where acres of pine had turned into a slurry, was still raw. Each year he returned to walk the stones and remember his last glimpse of her, stepping over a log. In his dreams, she always looks back, but here, he's never certain.

Chet Ensign writes in north New Jersey, where there are no bare hillsides yet.

Sparrow

Leaves rustle. A flutter of wings. Loud chirping can be heard from a nearby tree. A momma bird is calling out her encouragement. The baby sparrow makes its way to the edge of the nest and leaps.

Kim Lengling is an author and podcast host who regularly drinks coffee and chats with the critters that reside in her realm. *kimlenglingauthor.com*

On the Hills of Carabaku

I'm fumbling among the limestone blocks, full of nummulites and fossilized shells, scattered on the Dobrogean hills from Carabaku. Millions of years ago, in the Jurassic, these rocks lay beneath the brackish waters of the Thetis Sea. I'm fumbling on the bottom of the former sea Thetis.

Nicolae Dumitru is a retired mechanical engineer, born in Constanta, Romania.

Roach

I walk into the room and discover him, gasping, on the floor. "Oh," I say, "I thought I'd missed, but I gotcha!" I grab him by the antenna and haul him up to my face. "Apologies for making you suffer all night, old thing." I drop him into the disposal and another roach bites the dust.

Hannah Poole is a retired administrator loving her downsized apartment, little friends and all.

Pizza

I'm out getting pizza and I see a former coworker there. His face dirty, his clothes wrinkled. Was he homeless now? I turned away, hoping he wouldn't see me. Memories of our conflicts surface. I was obviously better off now. But he was the only one who got pizza.

When she's not writing books or articles, Dawn Colclasure can be found exploring the road less traveled or reading one of the many books to read that day. *dawnsbooks.com*

Dancing Leaves

My soul is bereaved of its loss. I walk into our bedroom, and I can no longer smell the fragrance of you. My heart aches. I glance out the window and see leaves spinning, circling upwards and dancing in the wind. It is then I feel the presence of you.

Jay Hernandez loves to read and occasionally pen a short story.

Life Laugh Dance!

Oh how we laughed! Oh how we danced! We laughed while we danced. We danced while we laughed. He came to the class every week. I didn't know who he was, where he was from, what he did. It was perfect. He didn't put a foot wrong.

Ellen Fox is an award-winning theatre playwright, who has also written for radio, film and television.

The Last Joy Ride

With it went away the impressions of my crazy rides, my baby's euphoric laugh when the air wooshed by his face. I looked on as the mechanic turned the corner, as Joy my eighteen-year-old scooter took its last ride to the garage.

Moutushi is a budding author, with two published books, and a voice-over artist, and she lives in Bangalore.

Predator Play

The little dude grabbed my head and pierced my earlobe with those tines he obsessively sharpens. He thought it was hilarious as he ran off with blood on his paws then laughed meowingly as he loped upstairs. Was I man or mouse? He didn't care: it was GOOD practice.

Firstly, Roger Barton is a musician and teacher terminally living in Frankfort, Illinois; lastly, verbal concision is not his forte but he is up to the challenge.

Paradise Found

Dressed in tweedy jacket, turn-ups and brogues, a battered, annotated book stuffed in his pocket, he clambered up the scaffolding, finding a secret vantage point overlooking the Dreaming Spires. In the afternoon sun, stretched out where no one could see him, he lost himself in Milton, deliriously happy.

Karen Jones can usually be found dreaming by the sea, seizing opportunities for adventures and loving the journey, dead ends and all.

Jean

Sitting, back to the door, staring at the wall, eating little, speaking to no one, mourning the death of his little girl, his first child. His jet-black hair turns silver as he searches the boundaries of his grief in a place where even his soul is hidden.

Jack Albert is a poet, student of history, and writer of small things.

Flushing Line 1942

Oblivious to the stifling heat pumping from beneath the car's tightly woven rattan seats, the coaches clattered across the borough, high above the roofs of the single-family homes and the four- and six-story apartment buildings built close to the street below, Genevieve felt as if she was floating.

Edward Di Gangi writes with a passion for people, place and discovery. *digangiauthor.com*

Vigil

"Count sheep," he said. "Never fails." But she kept losing count, backtracking, stressing. Now, she holds a tally counter, pressing its lever for each member of the wooly herd until her hand eventually falls slack with sleep. Beside her in the darkness, he listens; each click another water torture droplet.

Elizabeth Barton moves words around for fun and profit while living in Chicago with her husband, two cats, and more than a little self-doubt. *lizardesquewordpress.com*

The Boat

Mrs. S's son used to row a boat to the middle of the lake and sit there for hours "just thinking." Since he was only a teenager, Mrs. S was quite concerned. It didn't seem normal, she said. She was right. One day he rowed away and never came back.

Richard Evanoff is active in literary circles in Tokyo, Japan as a writer and performer.

Hospitality

"Will you have family over this Thanksgiving?" asks Latasha. Cappella shrugged, "They invite themselves to my Thanksgiving." "I will have no guests. My new apartment is unfurnished." "If my people hear I am fixing the dinner, they will all show up and, if necessary, eat on the floor," Cappella replies.

Steve Bailey lives in Richmond, Virginia and writes. *vamarcopolo.blogspot.com*

Koan

What was that noise? As soon as I stopped to listen, it stopped. Isn't that always the way? I went back to whisking the egg whites. There it was again, a flag beating in the wind. Eureka! I was applauding myself with the sound of one aging upper arm clapping.

Deborah Jones wanted to be a tugboat captain but, with some regret, chose broadcast news writing instead.

Music in the Morning

He plays Mozart in the morning. The notes flow through the house, down the hall, and stroke me awake. Then one night he played me while he was still asleep, fingers pressing my back slowly, then faster. I didn't know the notes but felt the music. Nine months later, crescendo!

Patti Cassidy adores Paris, film, and really good writing. Her radio plays, mostly noir, are on the web. *@Bostonplaycafe*

Queen Vashti

No. I will not dance naked before my husband and his courtiers. No. I will not submit. Yes, the men who compose sacred texts will malign and revile me. But yes, Queen Esther will succeed me. She will also refuse to obey the king. She will also rebel. And you?

Cordelia Frances Biddle wrote *They Believed They Were Safe.* *cordeliafrancesbiddle.net*

Birth Water

We are, my darling, a trail of being, we are a love that has forgotten the sky, we are a universe of our own. I love you so I don't forget I'm alive. You are the altar of my offering, you are the primordial water that gave birth to me.

Alexandru Cristian is a Romanian writer, historian, essayist, and poet who has authored several scientific papers. *@Alexand90060447*

Go Figure

Some days I am amazed by my own brilliance. On other days, I walk into walls, forget to release the park brake while driving, and miss my mouth when raising a cup to it to have a drink. "Had that mouth long?" ask my friends.

Natalie Bock is an ex-military, non-conformist theologian in training who regularly scribbles poetry and snippets of stories on any paper she can salvage from her handbag.

The Articulate "UM"

Talking Heads spew the airwaves with "um," but that simple morpheme is currently disguised with particular filler words. For example: Look! See! According to, Recently or Right? One favorite stalling phrase in vogue ... Let me be perfectly clear ...! Where is to "um" when only a momentary pause is required?

Deb Obermanns is an avid traveler, lover of storytelling, and international schoolteacher.

Co-Workers

On the first day of a job you meet people whose funerals you might one day attend. Emma shows you to the restroom. David retrieves your snack jammed in the vending machine. Years pass. So do they. In the receiving line you give thanks as their experience again precedes you.

Candace Tippett hikes and writes when nothing else makes sense. Instagram *@boonearang*

Address Book

I begin the process of calling mum's friends, to share the news. Her address book is coded.

"Flower lady."

"Moneybags."

"Army Dot."

My name is under "O."

"Our John."

The family, held together by Mum's pen.

"Our Colin."

"Our Alex."

I call "Our Adam":

A name not crossed out; yet.

John Holmes is a cyclist that writes and a writer that … *johnholmeswriter.com*

On Her Husband's Side

A man lying in bed was irritated because she was on his side of the bed asleep. Being tired, he asks her to move over so he could lay down. Loving her husband, she looked at him and said, "You can always count on me to be on your side."

Dr. Charles Gibson is a professional writer/editor who lives in Tennessee and holds an Education Doctorate in Leadership. LinkedIn *@charles-gibson*

Houdini Harnessed

Energized yet fatigued, the perfect combination for a toddler meltdown with a captive audience. Houdini restrained, frustrated but determined to ruin the morning commute in a last attempt to win over the crowd with his cries for freedom. Fifty minutes later, Houdini admits defeat to the stroller. Peace restored. Finally.

Dabbling with words, urban sketching and photography as Scott explores new cultures, experiences, and landscapes. Instagram *@scott.sketches*

Trials

Her attorney sucked on a mint, and she trembled. A nearby deputy exhaled, making her skin crawl. Just behind, a woman gulped coffee, and she fought the urge to jump the railing and strangle her. The judge entered and asked for her plea. Her attorney replied, “Insanity driven by misophonia.”

Shauna Lee Sanford McCarty is a retired educator who enjoys all kinds of wordplay.

When Stars Fell to Earth

The scream of butterflies was followed by the wilting of grasshoppers, and the silencing of cicadas. Stars gathered. Clouds gathered to ward them off. Stars descended en masse. Clouds enlisted thunder, lightning. Stars kept coming, their rain versus H_2O. The ensuing battle had no winners. In rain, hail, even snow.

Keith Hood is a writer and photographer who lives in Ann Arbor, Michigan.

Precognitive Dream

"Oh my gosh, how funny." The tarot lady puts on her cat eye-reading glasses. "What?" "I woke up this morning wondering why I dreamed of a random can of Coke." "Ha, I drink it all the time." "I never do." "I wish I had that power."

Adrian Voss enjoys exploring silence while sipping green tea and rarely hears her phone ring. *adrianvoss.com*

Once Upon a Time

Footprints in the dirt on a secluded country road lead to the dark timber house. There rests the painful existence of their forlorn childhoods. They call it Orphanage. Scumbling technique amplifies the opaque mood of her mind, as if keeping the memory alive would prevent them from falling into oblivion.

Amateur photographer and author of micro and flash fiction, Andrea Damic lives in Sydney, Australia, where she has her words published in several publications. Twitter *@damicandrea*

Bath

"Bathtime, sweetie." sang seventy-five-year-old grandma. "No! Grandma!" yelled two-year-old granddaughter. "But your clothes are off and the water is warm." "Only if you do." "I can't." "Why?" "I can't. Come on, get in." "Grandma! You have to!" Grandma paused, undressed and they stepped into together.

Rosanne Ehrlich's work has been published in *Persimmon Tree, Panoplyzine, The Voices Project, Quillkeeper's Press* and *Ballantine Books* among others.

Going

Shapes disperse in random along a road. Morning breaks onto the black canvas of the hours. As dust rises the singer is the last to leave, her cabaret strewn, her song fastened inside a million tears. The road, a line between ripened wheat, travels as far as time takes.

Jenny writes every day and makes abstract ceramics.

Seventh Chances

Mariko crashed through the door. “It didn’t work.” Cole frowned and adjusted the machine. “It’s on to plan G then,” he sighed. The machine hummed to life. The air shimmered. “Remember, you’re going farther back this time.” Mariko nodded. “Seventh time’s the charm,” she said, stepping through the portal.

Matt Warnock is always thinking about stories and what-ifs, and it gets pretty noisy in his head sometimes.

High Falls Lake #2

The forest air was heavy and still as daylight turned to dusk in the woods. The knock, knock, knock of a woodpecker, undisturbed by my presence as it picked at the bark of a dying loblolly was drowned out by the shrill squawk of a blue jay announcing my arrival.

Edward Di Gangi writes with a passion for people, place, and discovery. *digangiauthor.com*

On Lines that Prompt a Fuss & Bind Us

A man wearing no clothes runs in bare feet. His gait tracks a freshly painted line. “Is that his yellow brick road,” a young child asks with delight. “He’s no wizard,” his caretaker replies. “And this is no Oz. Let’s hope he doesn’t find himself in an unexpected fight.”

Jen Schneider is an educator who lives, works, and writes in small spaces throughout Pennsylvania.

Granddad

Granddad appeared larger than life, wealthy and of looming scorn. “That boy will never amount to anything,” I overheard him say about me to my mom. Dying penniless and alone, he now seems very small and my hurt shrouding his flimsy coffin is covered by the sod of his grave.

Jack Albert is a poet, student of history, and writer of small things.

I Am the Tie Around Joe's Neck

And you don't need to say anything. I can read it on your face. His wife packed me in his suitcase, traveling to present to the board. This is the career-maker, everything on the line. Well, except for their marriage. She's made clear where that stands. I'm just the messenger.

Chet Ensign writes in northern New Jersey where he has only one tie left and that one's not ugly.

Horse Nonsense

I don't care a piss for horses. At twelve, one dumped me down a mountain. Cactus pierced my ass, taking tweezers all night. Then a friend pushed me to another. "He's tame," she cheered. He refused to leave a water puddle. I'll stick to cats and dogs. Maybe a pig.

Soorya Townley is a copy editor and writer who lived in Cotonou, Benin and was the editor for the American Embassy newsletter.

Prospecting

I wake to find ten dollars under my pillow. All day, my tongue probes for potential cash, prodding each remaining tooth, hoping for a hint of wobbliness. Nothing budges. Daddy's dozed off on the couch. He's got loads of teeth! I sneak off to his workshop to find a hammer.

Elizabeth Barton moves words around for fun and profit while living in Chicago with her husband, two cats, and more than a little self-doubt. *lizardesque.wordpress.com*

Khala Najda

I was washing grapes today; you were by my side. You always made me smile, a rebellious Egyptian/Iraqi mix, dealt a difficult hand, diminished physically, but not intellectually, schooling me in feminism Arab style. Washing your grapes in Fairy liquid. *Khala means auntie and doesn't necessarily imply a blood/familial relationship.

Karen Jones can usually be found dreaming by the sea, seizing opportunities for adventures and loving the journey, dead ends and all.

Plastic Things

Touring my parents' new condo I asked, "Are you getting a pet?" Mom, a retired nurse who'd raised three daughters, said, "I'm not taking care of one more thing. I'd have plastic plants if I could." Dad nodded and said, "She'd have a mannequin for a husband if she could."

Kate Evans is author of *Call It Wonder*, winner of the Bisexual Book Award. *kateevanswriter.com*

Caring

Ahead, the fork. Loins tingling and senses pricked, I grab a guilty glance to the left. Musk, music, Bacchanalia. Longing. Life. I turn right, the misty path to the musty home. The door locked behind me, I call upstairs, "Home, Mum, the pharmacy had the right pads, this time."

N J Edmunds is a retired physician from Scotland, and his debut novel is *Miles Away* (Bear Press).

Pub of Sorrows

One definition of an Irish gentleman is someone who can sing "Danny Boy," but doesn't. He sang anyway. The clatter and hubbub lessened, some of us stared and listened, others attended their drinks. The rest continued conversations quietly. Soon, elation from the sad song's beauty's returned as always to ennui.

Firstly, Roger Barton is a musician and teacher terminally living in Frankfort, Illinois; lastly, verbal concision is not his forte but he is up to the challenge.

Family Closure

Her weathered house slippers stood outside the entryway. The family cat slumbered on them, occasionally meowing for attention. Their daughter's visits provided comfort, "Dad, Mum is gone." lovingly reminding her father, as she carried the slippers away. A tear rolled down his aged cheek, "I know," whispering his last words.

Deb Obermanns is an avid traveler, lover of storytelling, and international school teacher.

Dialogue Envy

I live in Minnesota, but I write stories set in my native Mississippi. A fellow novelist who was raised here in Minneapolis once told me that being from the South gave me an unfair advantage. She said, "In the South, people talk." As a Minnesotan, that's all she said.

At forty-five, Jonathan Odell walked away from his business at midlife, began writing and twenty-five years later, can't stop. Nor does he have any intention to.

Isn't She?

At last. He finally broke up with her and now he's mine. No more sneaking around. But sometimes I wonder if he's now seeing her on the sly. In fact, I'm almost sure of it. But I'm no longer the other woman. She is. Isn't she?

Roy Dorman enjoys reading and writing speculative fiction and poetry.

Part of Me

At hospice, I pull the window drapes open. The sun's rays descend upon her. I look at her lusterless eyes and frail smile. I kiss her. I whisper into her ear, "My love." And then she's gone, her spirit ascending the sun's rays, taking a part of me with her.

Jay Hernandez loves to read and occasionally pen a short story.

Historic Preservation

"Mommy," my young son approached me in the kitchen of our historic Boston home. "The man is in my bedroom again." "Is he a happy man or a sad man," I asked, paying more attention to the morning's news. "He doesn't have a head," Collin scoffed. "What do you think?"

Willa Bell is a poet who prefers the forest to real life.

Watery Planet

I used to be your watery planet. I carried you around inside me, my hands draped over the dome. My body, your terrarium. So forgive my confusion. Sometimes I forget you emerged. I act like you're still inside, bumping around without hands, a part inside me, short cord tethering you.

Nicole Brogdon is a trauma therapist in Austin, Texas, interested in strugglers and stories everywhere.

Entangled

Amber gazes at her mum's urn across the room with the lambent light continuing its perpetual dance. She wipes off her tears reminding herself to call an electrician. Saddened by the sight of her daughter's heartache, Mum's pellucid body scintillates under flickering light, not quite ready to let go yet.

Amateur photographer and author of micro and flash fiction, Andrea Damic of Sydney, Australia, has words published in *Friday Flash Fiction, Microfiction Monday*, among many others. Twitter *@DamicAndrea*

Soldiering On

The topped serving tray weighs heavily on her. Frying grease leaves an oily odor on her hair. Customer's rude remarks stick to her ribs. Her feet protest. Anger simmers within, threatening to bubble over at any time. But two young mouths to feed at home keep her in line.

Writing is Phil's love and creating micro fictions is his new passion.

Answers

As she leaned in to kiss me, she asked, "Why do you write poetry?" Then, she slipped off her shirt. After—hoping it works again, I wrote "I miss you—that's why." Later, she found the note. "Smart," she said, pulling me toward her with an acceptance better than *Ploughshares.*

Pasquale Trozzolo is a retired madman from Kansas and though his is work gets around, *Ploughshares* is still a no. *pasqualetrozzolo.com*

Competition

"Keep the noise down, I'm writing," John declared imperiously. Plugging in the Hoover Cheryl considered "Surviving Retirement" for her own competition entry. If she had time of course. "Can't you do that later? A cup of tea wouldn't go amiss." Cheryl scribbled furiously: "How to murder your husband."

Melanie lives in Devon, teaching music and writing to keep sane.

TerraSalis

Delivery sometimes required the less traveled route, a railroad track. His dog following, the boy satchel-shouldered morning papers. Pre-dawn darkness brought eerie chills, his old hound, whimpered away. An eyeless foggy face floated up, turned, drifted across the fields. Vision unexplained, fearing ridicule, the boy told no one.

Jack Albert is a poet, student of history, and writer of small things.

Beach Buggy Heaven

On a recent holiday in Ireland, I learned about the free buggy service at the nearby strand—I could hardly contain my excitement. For my wheelchair-bound son bouncing over the sand and being driven into the waves with seagulls crying overhead was far more magical than any trip to Disney.

Rosie Cullen lives in Manchester, UK, and likes writing all kinds of little stuff but still loves her big novel *The Lucky Country* best. *rmcullenauthor.wordpress.com*

Destiny

She'd planned her summer excitedly. Long, productive mornings in her garden office, writing her masterpiece; afternoons crafting, singing happily, reading. Sea swims, sunshiny chats, evening meals, strolls. But the room remained constantly locked, unentered, as life tumbled brutally, unexpectedly, down around her. The Tower had been her unheeded warning.

Karen Jones can usually be found dreaming by the sea, seizing opportunities for adventures and loving the journey, dead ends and all.

Let's Get Naked

Had we peaked that first-time, over three decades ago? Our mid-life sex had become mundane. We survived mid-life, scarred, resilient, but our desires sparked. Let's toss these pajamas! Let's get naked beneath these cool sheets—skin against skin, passion, peak, release. I have never loved you more.

Mary Schreiner lives in Wisconsin; she enjoys pine forests and the way corn fields wither in fall. Facebook *@maryschreiner*

Farewell

The sting of saltwater fills my eyes and washes my cheeks. The sweet smell of carnations fills the air. I see only tranquility resting in a sea of white satin and I exhale. Finally, you are at rest. Farewell to pain, farewell to fear, farewell dear friend.

Barbara Elliott is a Philadelphia-based artist, writer, and lover of baseball.

Side by Side

I found the paper dated March 20, 1969, this year. The cartoon resides next to Dad's obituary. A worker informs his computer it can be replaced by humans, while the obit tells all that my father apparently died of "self-inflicted gunshot wounds." Comedy/Tragedy does nothing to mask the plural.

S. Barron Thompson resides in New Jersey and is the first in his family to both graduate college and live in a trailer park where he has found the greatest sense of community he's ever experienced.

The Wire

We sat waiting for pizza. Marisol's every word, laugh, gesture and facial expression, transmitted sharp current to our hearts via an invisible wire. If she wanted pizza, we wanted pizza. Then, Marisol French kissed the delivery boy. A sharp current surged and shorted out a wire only we could see.

Keith Hood is a writer and photographer who lives in Ann Arbor, Michigan.

Disappointment

"That's what disappointment feels like," a colleague said to a distraught child. Her tone was matter-of-fact. If only someone had said that to me, in the same way, subtext—disappointment, that's life, you're okay, deal. As humans we are always disappointing each other. Years of therapy, much less necessary.

Connie Biewald teaches and writes in Cambridge, Massachusetts and Matènwa, Haiti. *conniebiewald.com*

Goodnight, Sweetheart, Goodnight

After twelve years, no nails tapping on the floor. No greeting when I get home. "Sophie," I call. "Where are you baby?" Then I remember. The trip to the vet last week. The last time I held her. Wrapped her in her favorite quilt, sang the lullaby. "Goodnight, Sweetheart, Goodnight."

Eileen Vorbach Collins misses her sweet little dog. *eileenvorbachcollins.com*

Clowning Around

Everyone stopped laughing when the car pulled up and ten clowns tumbled out, pulling weapons from their oversize trousers. The jugglers didn't stand a chance. Yes, I was there when the Circus War started.

Matt Warnock is always thinking about stories and what-ifs. It gets pretty noisy in his head sometimes.

Drunken Pals and Pumpkins

I drive by that house. Spacious lawn claimed by ghouls. Witches wobble, tombstones teeter, pumpkins totter, fully inflated, electrically inebriated. Mylar corpses stretch like continents. Come evening, I am too late for the party. Goblins, skeletons, et al, collapsed in deflated chaos. Face-down, blown-out exhausted, waiting for tomorrow's encore.

Linda M. Romanowski is a non-fiction/poetry writer, and newly minted grandmother.

Heartburn

John shook his head. "Waddaya want from me, Beth?" he asked. "The truth," Beth whimpered, staring at her uneaten dinner. The kitchen suddenly felt too small for both of them. John stood and dumped his food into the trash. He kissed Beth's forehead. "I love you but ... let's get takeout."

Rita Riebel Mitchell writes in the Pinelands of South Jersey where she loves to cook good food. *ritariebelmitchell.com*

Pearls Before Swine I Love

"God is in control," I told her, again. "You can think whatever you want, vote any way you want. In the end He always wins, even if you're goofy enough to think He didn't." "You're such a hypocrite," she muttered. "Like everyone. Only I won't spend forever roasting in hell."

Rick Moore writes magazine articles, records original music, and does some acting while awaiting the Rapture in Nevada. Facebook *@rickmoore*

Fallen

From inside the taxi, I scanned the roof imagining a person's descent to the sidewalk below. Patches of impatiens in full bloom circled the trees from which roots buckled the sidewalk. Puddles of rain spread out on the cement resembling stains of soaked blood. A jumper again. Another one? ... again?

William T. Vandegrift, Jr. lives in New Jersey, and is a writer of fiction working on a memoir as well.

Cousins

Every summer they'd pile in their car, traveling from far away. I'd wait at Grandma's, hopping from foot to foot—asking how much longer. Dying for them to arrive. As their car finally crested the hill, my heart leapt with joy. A whole week of cousins! What could be better?

Melissa Miles is a children's book author, certified educator, registered nurse, and board chair of Superhero Success Foundation, Inc. Twitter *@melissajmiles*

The Deep Cut

On the morning train, she cringed when the noisy schoolboys boarded. At the next station, the boys quietly got off, and the tight grip strangling her heart and stomach loosened. "It was twenty years ago. They're not the same as those boys in school," she scolded her fear.

Erik is an attorney (nonpracticing by choice) who lives and teaches English in Japan and lives in the northernmost island of Hokkaido with his wife and dog.

Occupation

Enemy army advances as fighting continues. Allied soldiers scattered all around the muddy hilltop. Muffled screams of horror frozen in time. Looking at his masterpiece through thick bifocal glasses, he grins at the sight unfolding on the battlefield. With a steady stroke of a brush, his miniatures come to life.

Amateur photographer and author of micro and flash fiction, Andrea Damic who lives in Sydney, where she has her words published or forthcoming in *50 Give or Take*, among many other publications. Twitter *@damicandrea*

Prickly With a Soft Underside

He is a gritty guy toting a badge and gun. Together, we provide a security presence, advising and mentoring, occasionally venturing into our community. Facing adversity united, we appreciate our complementary talents, laughing in unison when a student whips us "the finger" as the last Friday school bus departs. Sweet!

Deb Obermanns is an avid traveler, lover of storytelling, and international schoolteacher.

Other Words

Rhonda told Otto they should see other people. In other words, it was over between them ...

– Was it my personality, Rhonda?

– Actually, it was, Otto.

– Oh, I thought it might be my looks.

– That's another word for it.

– So, it wasn't the money?

– That's another word for it, too, Otto ...

David Sydney is a physician from Newtown, PA.

Rituale Interrupit

Dog mews at the back door, starting the nightly ritual: dog dashes out, piddles, returns. Hedges shook next door as a dusty brown body emerged. The old coyote gave us an aloof glance, ignoring dog yelping, my shouting. Lopes over a low stone wall, vanishing behind. Dog piddled, ran inside.

Tom Keating is a writer who lives in Massachusetts and is the author of his Vietnam memoir, *Yesterday's Soldier*. *tomkeatingwriter.com*

What Was It

The television crew arrived within minutes. Filmed the body and severed hand. Had no time to interview the sheriff who hadn't formulated a report. The television anchor said they would provide more information as it became available. They didn't. The anchor called it an accident. I know it wasn't.

Thomas Elson's stories appear in numerous venues: *Ellipsis*, *Flash Frontier*, and *North Dakota Quarterly*.

Morning Meeting

I meet her in the park every morning. Before blessing her, she raised her right hand above her head, shouting cheerfully: "Today I feel wonderful, the doctors told me that I am in remission!" I walk towards her, thinking: *I believe that* and I'll confess how much I love her!

Nicolae Dumitru is a retired mechanical diplomat and an engineer and writer from Constanta City, Romania.

Someone Should Have Objected at the Wedding

My sister. Who knew me best. Aunt Quincy. Who suspected the worst. My ex-boyfriend. Who was supposed to show up. Did he really not want to have kids? I actually don't want to have them either. All that my new husband and I have in common is this huge mistake.

Shoshauna enjoys how life presents stories all over the place.

Duvet Day

I heard the phrase "duvet day" on a tv show and have since hankered for one. A day of blissful rest under my quilt with a good book and the TV remote to binge watch. Not to be disturbed by anyone or anything for a whole day! Guess I can dream.

Alison Davidson is a Brit living in New Jersey with a passion for dogs, hiking, and now writing!

Sisters

We spotted the skirt at the same time. Bold, bright, bohemian blocks, designed to draw attention to the wearer. Together we exclaimed, "Look at that skirt!" She ended her sentence with "I'd never wear it; everyone would look at me." I echoed her last five words, but with delight.

Natalie Bock is an ex-military, non-conformist theologian in training who regularly scribbles poetry and snippets of stories on any paper she can salvage from her handbag.

As We Retreat they March Onwards

Out of darkness wanders dayglo yellow reflecting rain bubbles on the tarmac. Cars motionless now. Inside faces peer black. The light sweeps side to side, piercing windows for souls. Beside me he gurgles, bubbles rising like alarms. Our hands touch, I grip. Everything runs through me—his life, aspirations, everything.

AN Grace lives in Liverpool, England where his short fiction and poetry has appeared or is forthcoming in *Queen's Quarterly*, *Seize The Press*, *Fifth Estate*, *Free Inquiry* and many others. Twitter *@thisisnboring*

Second Chances

I broke her heart, but God gives us second chances. She is at a streetlight, in a new car next to mine. I stalk her into Dunkin Donuts and apologize. She's mad, won't speak. Her girlfriend is watching. I drive away. Deciding to call her anyway. Paper floating in driveway.

Christopher Michael Blake is from the New Jersey shore and is the author of the horror novel, *Prey for Dawn* and the mystery novella, *The Cape May Murders*. *christophermichaelblake.com*

Random Song

Connor's big brother stays up eating pizza and plays blistering electric guitar until 4 a.m. every night. He shreds the same song over and over ("Marry Me," the #1 wedding song of 2009), then crashes until afternoon. Wait, sorry: I meant Connor's dad, not big brother. Connor's mom died in June.

Robb Lanum is a failed screenwriter in Los Angeles who fell in love with the short form.

The Box of Shadows

A story mysteriously contained within this olden wooden box. A box where echos gave voice to the shadows that lurked. A box sealed by archaic wisdom. Inscribed on the top of this quaint box, a message or caution that read, WITHIN WITHOUT INSIDE OUT RISE OR FALL I KNOW ALL.

Katrenia Busch is an award-winning poet and published writer.

Hope

When I lost them both in the wreck, I heard at least a thousand clichés about hope. Every platitude. Every condolence. There's a ton of them. Believe me. Still, even in this darkness I cling to hope. Knowing that the moment I let go, I'll never find my way back.

Melissa Miles is a children's book author, certified educator, registered nurse, and board chair of Superhero Success Foundation, Inc. Twitter *@melissajmiles*

The Apiary

Hallway clock chimes Papa's spirit through Thin Places. In his room, sheltered from gentle rains, looking across his fields we mourn. The sextant's chapel toll, word to friends many and foes few, our grandsire is dead. True knowing though is incomplete, who will tell his bees?

Jack Albert is a poet, student of history, and writer of small things.

In Support of Ghosts

My childhood home, my memories sold. I stood there in silence amongst moldy magazines, faded pictures, and ghosts—who protected me when she was drunk, when she tried to silence my laughter with insults. My mother, laughing in that picture. My ghosts, encouraging me to toss it in the trash.

Mary Schreiner lives in Green Bay, Wisconsin. She enjoys pine forests, and the way corn fields wither in fall. Facebook *@maryschreiner*

Dental Symphony

The maestro huffs and grunts, and upside down, mouth agape, I hear the scritch, scratch, scrape of the dental symphony. "Bite and grind and open." The assistant spies an imperfection, and the screeching burr shrieks its lyric aria. "Rinse and close. I'll see you next summer," elicit a standing ovation.

Tony Tinsley is a professor emeritus of psychology and an author and editor who divides his time between the Pacific Northwest and the heartland in the United States.

Nostalgia

I flip the first two pancakes, which never turn out right. I'll eat them. I hear the words, "Snow!" and "Pancakes!" The kids won't be long now. A petal falls from the last flower I picked a few days ago. Winter has arrived and I think of Mom.

Bish Denham grew up in the US Virgin Islands and is the author of three children's books and numerous articles. Facebook *@bishdenham*

The Emperor Wears No Clothes

The pine trees looked enviously at their neighbors, the deciduous trees in their resplendent red, yellow, and orange, "Dressed for the autumn ball?" "Don't be jealous. Soon we will be shedding all this opulence and be as naked as the Emperor with no clothes. Be content with your evergreen."

Kwan Kew Lai is an author, a Harvard medical faculty physician, an infectious disease specialist, a disaster response volunteer, an artist, and a runner. *kwankewlai.com*

Catch!

In my agony, I imagined flinging the ten-pound exercise ball at the smug young trainer, confident Todd couldn't catch it. I'd show him this aging athlete could still sling his glory despite a bad back. Instead, the ball dropped on my foot scoring me another two months of physical therapy.

Marc Littman is a prolific short story and novel writer and playwright who writes from painful personal experience.

Cough

Why is he here, sitting tall, like a galleon surrounded by wrecks? I cough and he turns his head. A name is called. A creased-up man shuffles towards the doctor's door. Then it's me. Movement forces out another cough. He's watching with that stare of contempt the healthy have perfected.

John is not sure whether he's a cyclist who writes or a writer who cycles.

My Bob

The way you looked at me backstage years later was different than the way you looked at me when we first met. A shift, a jolt, a thundering gaze from your oceanic irises. I put my hand on yours backstage, but then pulled it away quickly. Some storms are detrimental.

Elaina writes, doodles, and thinks about ways to travel without leaving her house.

Two As in Wawa

After twelve regretful steps I open the door to the Wawa. I pass the counter where the price of cigarettes makes you wonder why smokers don't choose pot. I stand in front of the cooler, fighting then surrendering to my urge. Fuck it! *Redbulls Two for $4.50.*

S. Barron Thompson resides in New Jersey and is the first in his family to both graduate college and live in a trailer park where he has found the greatest sense of community he's ever experienced.

Put on Your Own Oxygen Mask Before Helping Others

But how when the world is overflowing with stupid and your mom's dying and your child's called mop-boy at school although she's a girl and beautiful to you? And you promised you wouldn't, but you ate three cookies before your first coffee. And your clients' problems make your life sound daydreamy?

Amy Marques penned children's books, barely read medical papers, and letters before turning to short fiction. *amybookwhisperer.wordpress.com*

Guess How Much

Helen learned to pinch pennies from her widowed mother in their shtetl in Poland. An immigrant after the Holocaust, she honed her frugality. Toys were few but food was plentiful. Years passed. Helen displayed another bargain. "Guess how much," she challenged. Her grandson's price shockingly low, Helen scowled, then chuckled.

Janet Hiller is a textbook author and pastel artist who loves to read and write poetry and creative nonfiction.

Winter

Hues of sparkling gold and red abound, reflecting the sunlight. The colors appear slowly yet fade fast. Then days grow short and nights long. Cold creeps into my bones. With my belly full, I lumber to my lair to slumber. See you in the spring.

Married, Catherine is a retired investment banker, competitive equestrian, yoga teacher, aspiring writer and lover of animals. *catherinerochester.com*

Double Trouble

Dad made me drive the gravel backroads to Crystal's house. He didn't want me sharing the main roads with "all those crazies," plus it'd slow me down. Crystal's dad said no backroads. If we ran into trouble, who'd be there to help? So, we took both; trouble was a given.

Chet Ensign writes in northern New Jersey, right where the paved roads end.

Showdown

A single mother with a figure already announcing the approach of middle age, she understands she's no longer "a catch." Still, she bravely holds her chin out, her lips in a tight, straight line, trying to show that she is less vulnerable. More fierce than the man realizes.

Ed DiGangi writes with a passion for people, place, and discovery. *digangiauthor.com*

Perspective

My son is the same age as when my husband and I married. When my kids were little, I used to wonder who they'd become at each stage. But it's all theoretical then. Now my kids are grown, and I see them clearly at every age they ever were.

A special education teacher by day, Theresa Milstein writes middle grade, YA, and dabbles in poetry. *theresamilstein.blogspot.com*

Autumn Storm

The storm creates a stream in the gutter, occasionally backing up with leaves. Suddenly I'm building dams in the woods behind our house, creating byways and tributaries in the stream, the smell of moist earth and decaying leaves strong in my nostrils. I control the urge to get a stick and play.

Hannah Poole dabbles in memoir and music libraries when not scuffing leaves along the pavement.

Acrobats

I drink my coffee and watch the circus. Squirrels feast on Yaupon berries while hanging by their hind feet. Jays swoop in to sip from the birdbath then splash a bit. A mockingbird practices his Karate moves against the window pane. When the show is over, I start my day.

Mary Janicke is a gardener and writer living in Houston, Texas.

Vignettes

I remember our red-shingled, four-room house on Locust Street, the bathroom door creaking open as I emerged. I remember Mom's friend Azalea's arm around my twelve-year-old shoulders, steering me to the bedroom door. I remember Mom asleep, curled toward the wall. And Azalea's voice, Southern, soft: Go say goodbye.

Casey Mulligan Walsh is a former speech-language pathologist and writer who lives with her husband Kevin and two feisty cats in upstate New York. *caseymulliganwalsh.com*

Sea Life

These days, spent alone by the ocean, have changed me, numbed my edges, like my collected beach detritus: weathered driftwood, gull-pecked moon shells, blurry seaglass as smooth and pale as the sky. But like the living creatures, a creeping crab or slimy snail, I'm also filled with determination and possibility.

Diane lives, writes, and teaches by the beach north of Boston where she has been published in *AARP The Ethel*, *Boston Globe Connections*, *HuffPost*, and elsewhere. *dianeforman.com*

Status Symbol

Jim was grateful for the email message from the literary magazine rejecting his submission, but poignantly aware of his status as a neophyte. Renowned authors boasted of rejections using numbers from NBA basketball scores. Eager to validate his status as a writer, Jim immediately began work on his second rejection.

Tony Tinsley is a professor emeritus of psychology and an author and editor who divides his time between the Pacific Northwest and the heartland in the United States.

Why

The Genius at the Bar failed to reconnect us. We exchange knowing glances, but you're inaccessible; trapped in a dead zone that no longer responds to my touch. Friends say I'm only down a letter, but I've lost a co-conspirator, a consonant and, sometimes, a vowel.

S. Barron Thompson resides in New Jersey and is the first in his family to both graduate college and live in a trailer park where he has found the greatest sense of community he's ever experienced.

Words

You find me, again and again. I wander through your gallery and flirt for your attention. My shoulders collapse as she secures your arm. I'm ordinary, she's a catch. Indecision walks with you. I watch you edit her for me. You're charmed by my simplicity. Forever, until you meet another.

Adeel Khan from the UK, studying a BA (Hons) English literature and creative writing degree. Twitter *@AdeelKwrites*

Kids on Fire

The kids are on fire, it's 4 a.m., and you roll another cigarette the music so loud no one is talking to each other. We haven't said a word for hours. What did we do with so much time? All that drinking doesn't age well, you know. I know, I know.

Georgia May is a part-time film journalist for various online platforms with several online and paperback poetry publications. *georgiamayfilms.com*

Pauline

"I want you to kill me. I've had enough!" Pauline, lupus, sickle cell and a hole in her heart, hands Leah a pillow. Leah grips it tightly, takes a deep breath, holds the pillow above Pauline's face. A passing night-nurse looks in, "Everything alright?" Pauline looking at Leah, "Everything's fine."

Ellen Fox is an award-winning playwright, who has also written for radio, film, and television.

Lost

Clyde, cousin and buddy, quietly returned from the Great War. Meeting horror I pray never to encounter, he survived battles, but not the demons of his Flanders conflicts. Lost in war's fog of trenches and death, poisoned by hateful drunken spirits, he returned, but never came back.

Jack Albert is a poet, student of history, writer of small things.

An Erroneous Assumption

Aunt Vira was 102. I texted her and asked to visit but copied her granddaughter—assuming she would give her the message. Vira replied immediately: "Please visit anytime except: Wednesdays and Thursdays are my meetings and Sundays are church. BTW, my granddaughter does not know my schedule!"

Mary Schreiner lives in Green Bay, Wisconsin where she enjoys pine forests and the way corn fields wither in fall.

Canyon

His horse went wild-eyed, ears pricked at the screams from the sand-scoured bones of dead ponies echoing against the canyon walls. Sounds that only a horse could hear. Though he himself somewhat spooked by the silence, and cold without knowing why as he rides the terrain that keeps the corpses.

Pamela Ryder is the author of two novels in stories and a short story collection. *pamelaryder.com*

Then and Now

When we first dated, we'd go to those indoor arcades on the boardwalk. Skee-ball is my favorite while yours is air hockey. We'd win ribbons of tickets. Now, "tickets" go on a card. When we give our winnings to a random kid, their faces still light up the same.

A special education teacher by day, Theresa Milstein writes middle grade, YA, and dabbles in poetry. *theresamilstein.blogspot.com*

The Medication

"Take one of these, young one. It won't get you out of Wonderland, but it will help you sleep through the evil that lurks in the shadows at night," said the strange man in the purple hat. "I've been taking them for years, and I'm fine."

Kym Payne is currently studying towards a degree in creative writing, and she is very active on TikTok. *@libraryofkym*

The Year We Parted

In balmy spring I denied it. Earth was blooming; so was I. He would surely come home. Hot summer brought lawyers' letters. Enraged, I chopped the rosebushes down. Golden autumn shimmered as we negotiated terms. I gave birth to our child alone. Then melancholy winter descended. My grieving season began.

K Roberts is a professional nonfiction writer, a published artist, and a first reader in fiction at the Canadian magazine *Nunum*.

The Season

Each night, deer enter the yard to eat the corn set out for them. Such beautiful creatures and so peaceful to watch. The woman smiles as she watches them, filled with love for these graceful creatures. A shot rings out. Hunting season has begun.

Kim's days are filled with written and spoken words; writing, podcasting and talking with the critters who reside in her realm. *kimlenglingauthor.com*

Creationists

"We're goddesses," whispered Jo. "Making life." Lisa adjusted the lightning rod. "Yeah, right sis." Polycarbonate bones and graphene sinews, his torso glistened under the lights: broad shoulders, buns of steel, generously proportioned where it mattered. Jo's hands were clammy; Lisa licked her lips. Tonight, they'd make a man of him.

Alastair Millar is an archaeologist by training and a translator by trade; he lives in the Czech Republic. *linktr.ee/alastairmillar*

Watch Ending

Detective Jenkins sat in his gray Cutlass outside the dilapidated building. Solemnly swirling the last of his coffee with artificial sweetener in its Styrofoam cup, he makes his decision. When the suspect emerges Jenkins will arrest him, book him at the precinct, and head to Vegas with the confiscated cash.

Michael Janicke is a musician and school bus driver living in Wilton, New York.

Epiphany

The cook, the house, and the cat. Familiars in a weathered niche, growing old in isolation. She supplicant, he reclusive, set within a construct of inadequacy. At the eleventh hour she realized! The cook told the house, then the cat, and took to the hills in her yellow car.

Jenny is a published writer based in the UK where she also makes abstract ceramics.

The AGA

In the Facebook post it gleamed. I can see why you wanted to post a photo of a ridiculously expensive oven that has just been professionally cleaned. Your pride of the kitchen. A beautiful thing. Oh, to have wealth like that, for an oven made for cooking, that gets treated like a queen.

Alison Davidson is a Brit living in New Jersey with a passion for dogs, hiking, and now writing!

Lonely

Widowed. She moved into the in-law section of her son's house and, walking the dog in the new neighborhood, encountered a handsome man her age on a walk. They talked. She liked him. Two days later, she saw him again, walking hand-in-hand with his wife. Lonely again.

Steve Bailey lives in Richmond, Virginia, where he writes.

The Russians are Coming

"Damn! I broke the wine bottle," said Borysko. "Do we have another container?" "We might in the cellar," said Mykola. So they ransacked some storage shelves downstairs for a conflagration tool. I opened the door. I heard, "Grygory, here! Throw it! Now!" Then I launched the flaming vinegar bottle tankward.

Firstly, Roger Barton is a musician and teacher terminally living in Frankfort, Illinois; lastly, verbal concision is not his forte, but he is up to the challenge.

The Trip

Andrei leaves Enschede by bicycle, on a trip to Germany. He crosses the border between Holland and Germany, thinking, almost instantly, of his grandparents who had lived entire their lives beyond the Iron Curtain—between the closed borders of communist Romania ruled by an odious dictatorship.

Nicolae Dumitru is a retired mechanical engineer born in Constanta, Romania.

Butterfly

I was working in my front yard when a beautiful butterfly flew past. The bright red butterfly was something new to me. Out of nowhere a bird flew by and ate it. Couldn't say what kind, I'm not a birdologist. It is true; nature is sharp of claw and beak.

Doug Hawley is a retired actuary who writes, hikes, and volunteers.
sites.google.com/site/aberrantword/hello

A Perfect Relationship

"Couples get everything, right?" The woman in the bus queue grasps his arm. Finn turns, putting the sleet to his back. "Let's pretend we're one, and swap warming up." She nods to a cafe. But when the bus comes, she won't give her number. "Why ruin things?" Her kiss, warm.

Paul Many has left New York for US flyover country. So far no one seems to be gaining on him. *amazon.com/Paul-Many*

Everything I Needed to Know About Parenting, I Learned on the Chicago "L"

From the Loop elevated, I saw a mother hurrying on Lake Street below while her toddler lagged behind. Would she snatch the kid, angrily hoisting her to a hip? No. She squatted and held out her arms. The child flew in, laughing! A lift, a kiss, and they hurried on.

Deborah Jones wanted to be a tugboat captain but, with some regret, chose broadcast news writing instead.

Union County

A peaceful soul, Absalom loved walking Union County's hills. Visiting his daughter's home there, he suddenly became ill. Staying the night, attempting sleep, mare's nest memories of wartime imprisonment recaptured him. Plundering his aging heart, death embraced Absalom, releasing his peaceful soul to Union County's hills.

Jack Albert is a poet, student of history, writer of small things.

Attracting the Butterfly

Flitting back and forth behind the counter, the young woman in the pink uniform serves coffee and doughnuts in exchange for smiles and change. Every night the customer adds sweet liqueur to his coffee and sips. Catching a whiff of the familiar scent, she sighs, hoping he stays until closing.

Rita Riebel Mitchell writes little pieces of fiction every day. *rrmitchell.com*

Fishing for Answers

Grief is a slippery fish. I'm just carrying out the business of life when I'm blindsided with a flash of vivid memory just like it happens in movies and on TV. What then? Keep wading through water? Or wallow underneath until I'm ready to breathe again?

A special education teacher by day, Theresa Milstein writes middle grade, YA, and dabbles in poetry. *theresamilstein.blogspot.com*

The Rally

Yesterday, our elderly mother was herself again—talking, laughing. She announced her desire to live, a turnaround from prior, not wanting to hurt us. Our spirits soared. She passed this morning, her still body lost to her wishes. The nurse called it a Rally. To us, it seemed ... so cruel.

Philip Goldberg's passion is fiction, from micro to short stories, many of which have been published.

Morning

Sunlight beams through the window, waking me. I stretch in a downward-facing dog yoga pose, then prance downstairs to eat breakfast. After, I groom myself and go to my toilet. I play chase with Dog. Exhausted, I perch on the back of my armchair, purr and return to slumber.

Married, Catherine is a retired investment banker, competitive equestrian, yoga teacher, aspiring writer, and lover of animals. *catherinerochester.com*

The Mentor

On winter afternoons, when dark descended early, your office, in the bowels of the building: subtle lamplight, tasteful, inviting. A middle-aged latecomer to Law, success made you generous, with time and advice. But elegant, refined femininity belied incisive intelligence and fearless sentencing. An iron fist in a velvet glove indeed.

Karen Jones can usually be found dreaming by the sea, seizing opportunities for adventures and loving the journey, dead ends and all.

Dad

How many fathers teach their daughters to change a flat, check the oil, etc., before they learn to drive? More than once we tried to pin him down. "Didn't you want a son?" He just smiled. "All I wanted to know is if you had ten fingers and ten toes."

Bish Denham grew up in the US Virgin Islands and is the author of three children's books and numerous articles. Facebook *@bishdenham*

Time Out

Leaves fall slowly. He feels before he sees. There's a sudden gossamer of breath and, SNAP, a twig cracks. As he turns, the pendulum swings, it's clear what this is. In the last second before the clock strikes the hour ... His whole life before him. There's never time, never time.

Laura Cooney is a writer from Edinburgh with some recent publications. *lozzawriting.com*

Whole Bagel

Once she's out of sight with the dog, I slip through the open door. It's all there—bagel, strawberries, juice. I take half the bagel and leave before the girl comes downstairs. Someday she'll ask her mom: why can't I have a whole bagel? Then, no breakfast for me.

Emmy-award-winner Amy Bass is a writer, professor, and sport thinker. *amybass.net*

Sharper Than Obsidian

Scientists swear obsidian is the sharpest cutting edge in the world—over five hundred times sharper than steel blades. As Shelby wrote her husband's obituary, she knew science had it all wrong. In fact, she highlighted a few of Jack's scathing traits that had cut her with much more precision.

Melissa Miles is a children's book author, certified educator, registered nurse, and board chair of Superhero Success Foundation, Inc. Twitter *@melissajmiles*

Rock Scramble

Where do I step, what to hold? A man speaking Czech extends a hand. Without pride, I grab it. He supports my weight—never again. Springing ahead, I'd rather be caught from below than dragged up. Summit reached, above the birds, photos taken. Now, how do I get down?

Jacquelyn Burke likes space travel is a little bit nerdy, but mostly awesome.

Celebration?

Last year I celebrated my retirement—no more having to face those miserable Monday mornings, impossible deadlines, and nasty office politics. Today I stopped celebrating because I have been facing something much more difficult: myself.

Mary Schreiner lives in Green Bay, Wisconsin. She enjoys pine forests and the way corn fields wither in fall. Facebook *@MarySchreiner*

Taking Care

Nothing but splint between her foot and her knee. She was limping but leading us on. Someone walked the old woman to her house by the sea. The man didn't let her go till she was inside. Then it was I deciding to lock it or leave it ajar.

Karen S. Henry, author of *All Will Fall Away,* writes poetry and soon hopes to help young children in Boston learn to read. *finishinglinepress.com/product/all-will-fall-away-by-karen-s-henry*

Rush Hour

Ah, rush hour! Shrouded in deep morning gloom, behind a line of cars, stalled at the traffic light. Look! Twinkling red lights, vining around the glossy spikes of the school yard fence. What, they're putting up Christmas decorations already? It's not even Thanksgiving yet! But no—just the reflections of a thousand angry taillights.

Michaele Jordan (believes she's a bit odd), was born in LA, educated in New York, and lives in Cincinnati where she's worked at a kennel, a Hebrew School and AT&T.

Ringing Bells

The ship sounds six bells as its anchor splashes into the bay. She listens from her widow's walk, black hair and full-length deep-green dress flowing out behind her in the ocean breeze. It has been so long. "Stop ringing that damn ship's bell," she says softly, "and come ring mine."

Steve Bailey lives in Richmond, Virginia, where he writes and, once in a while, gets published.

Who Needs a Blender?

Take the frivolous woman and discard the Haute couture, the costly cosmetics meticulously applied to create a superficial appearance and the coiffuring hair highlights. All that remains is a doltish and anonymous skeletal framework. Much like a blender, it generates noise, occupies valuable space and is totally unnecessary.

Franco Manna is an international educator who loves languages, beach sunsets and spending time with his beautiful daughters. Instagram *@francomanna29*

The Burbs

Why do I detest my hometown, its manicured lawns adorned by patriotic exclamations, its monotony of garrison-colonials, and raised-ranches, its patterns of vinyl siding and shingle roof? Could it be only the uncomfortable sofa I wish to forget? The one mother reupholstered over and over, stiff-backed and tear-stained?

Brian Pilling is an author and poet based in Cape Cod, MA.

City

She only ever came here on holidays, this was a carefree place, this city suggested that adventures will have no consequences. Surely she deserved an adventure? These smirking eyes, this smile tempted, beckoned ... Would she regret it later? Only one way to find out. She leaned in for a kiss.

Alex Keesh loves books, cats, coffee and walks, and hopes to become a published author someday. Twitter *@keesh_alex*

Hey, Dreamer

With deep gratitude for being known, I listen to the lyrics, get lost in the beauty of the music and strong accent that speaks to my Celtic soul. Sent as an offering of love by a new friend, at a time of great change, it's the soundtrack to my new life.

Karen Jones can usually be found dreaming by the sea, seizing opportunities for adventures and loving the journey, dead ends and all.

Sacred Spaces

There are only you and your god(s) in the sacred space. Maybe trees, a mountaintop, a view of the sea. Alone: you build a shrine; give thanks; leave offerings. Shared: pilgrims follow. Merchants know travelers need rest, nourishment. Souvenirs. Your sacred space, now a venue, is thirsty for tourists.

Eve is a librarian, storyteller, poet, mother of four adult children, keeper of a good dog, a bad cat, and spouse of husband who keeps bees.

Last Moments

Their last moments, like the string of pearls given on her 30th anniversary. His breathing, labored, escapes as a final faint retreat. An obstinate spirit shriveled against the incursion of a relentless disease. She holds his hand. Outside remained just that, reaching to the edge of their universe and beyond.

S.D. Brown lives in Dorset, England where he writes poetry, shorts stories and novellas, and has been published in *Acclaim*, *Platform for Prose* and *The Fortnightly Review*.

"X" DAY (975)

He found himself surrounded by a blinding white light. He was making chaotic movements and did not understand where he was and why. He didn't know even who he was! In the memory of time, this day was for him identical to the first day or to the last day.

Nicolae Dumitru is a retired mechanical engineer born in Constanta, Romania.

Domesticated Wilderness

They married in a tiny church in the back throat of a holler, where she'd picked blackberries and he'd chopped wood, where they found each other through curtains of wild brush in the shadows of mountains, where beasts slept, where they hunted for light and found it in each other.

Melanie Maggard is a Seattle-based flash fiction and flash CNF writer who loves drabbles and lives for Champagne, popcorn, and peanut butter. *melaniemaggard.com*

Chomp Chomp

She was known to chew on everything—her cuticles, leather chairs, bubblegum, necks. If it smelled like apples, lust, or Christmas, she'd bite. But now that she is a grown up, she's wiser—chews on parenthood, aging, and lots of carrots. *Chew on this*: you never have to remind her.

Elaina is a writer, an ice cream lover, and watches too many reruns. *elainawrites.com*

Last Call to Board

Last call to board. And yet here I sit. Frozen. Running to or from? Pursuit or escape. Sunrise. Sunset. Standing up means life starts over again. Unknown. Greener? Does the freedom to fail outweigh a comfortable life of emptiness? Safety. Hope. Last call to board. I breathe—and I rise.

Terrence is an aspiring author in Ohio who is feeling grateful. *terrencelitwiller.com*

Mirror Be Damned

Mirror be damned, the image was wrong; like that of the long-deceased father. Clutches the phone, "Just Cuts? I'd like a cut and color." Following day, after a sensuous night at Dance 41, they overdosed. Dead, unlike anyone familial. Now their true self; coif-fured; earrings; rouge; lipstick. No person, no mirror could mock them any longer.

Chris Lihou is retired and trying to find deeper understanding via writing; mostly poetry.

Dreaming

A glass ball falling, a crystal orb shattering. Thousands of kaleidoscopic shards pierce my skin. I am jolted awake. Tears streaming down my face, I gasp for air. Camelot is broken beyond repair, and I am left standing amid the ruins. Alone.

Bish Denham grew up in the US Virgin Islands and is the author of three children's books and numerous articles. Facebook *@bishdenham*

Her Best Feature

She always hated her ears, which she felt were too large. And she was never comfortable with her chunky legs and stubby toes. But her trunk, oh, how she loved her trunk. A trunk that could get to leaves only the giraffes could reach.

Roy Dorman enjoys reading and writing speculative fiction and poetry.

Hawk

A red-tailed hawk gives a screech as it takes flight from a tree branch. His feathers glisten in the rising sun, reflecting the colors of orange and gold. With a sharp turn and talons outstretched, he dives toward the ground. Swoop and grab. Breakfast is served.

Kim Lengling is an author and likes to chat with the critters that reside in her realm. *kimlenglingauthor.com*

Only One Shot at Life

Holding my mother's wrinkly hand, I said, in another life, in another world, I'd like to reverse the roles. I would make sure my daughter would have a job, no abusive husband, and a life worth living. Smiling vaguely, she said, *what if we get only one shot at life?*

Marzia Rahman is a Bangladeshi writer who writes flashes in the morning and dreams of flashes at night. Twitter *@MarziaR57167805*

Angel

Rex sucked through the melted-out vodka miniature. Beautiful dirty white light spread through him. Red Bull Gives You Wings. He laughed at the image of himself as an angel; and then stopped as the wings were wilting, the light already dimming. He flicked the flame so he could see.

Rory Hughes is a South London-based writer and music journalist. He can be found on Twitter *@RoryHughesBooks*

On a Daily Dose of Pea(ce)s (and Wonder)

"You can't get There from Here—potholes are perilous. Pretzels lack salt," said the pigeon as it pecked a toilet in the park. "Where's There?" another asked, worried the toilet might flush (pigeons easily plucked). "It's a place of pea(ce)s," the pigeon replied. "And a loaf of Wonder."

Jen Schneider is an educator who lives, works, and writes in small spaces throughout Pennsylvania.

The Last Time

I remember the first time: I ate bacon; I boarded an airplane; we kissed. Memory saves a first; we know we never did it before. I can't recall the last time: I ate a homegrown tomato; I rode the subway; we made love. Memory bypasses a last; we don't know we'll never do it again.

Ann S. Epstein writes novels, stories, and memoir and is herself as short and provocative as microfiction. ***asewovenwords.com***

Still

Everything is still. The building is quiet. Few cars are on the highway, and it's too dark for boats to be on the river. The water is smooth, but the currents swirl like smudges on a mirror—shattered by the reflection of the moon and the stars.

Ed DiGangi writes with a passion for people, place, and discovery. ***digangiauthor.com***

Capes Clause

"Yes, I see the Capes Clause on your policy." "I understand General Mayhem blasted your garage to Dimension X. You still need to fill out form 13-C." "No, I don't know if you can sue the Justice Squad for negligence." "We'll send an adjuster once the space slugs are contained.

Matt Warnock is always thinking about stories and what-ifs, and it gets pretty noisy in his head sometimes.

The Bird Man

When he bent over to tie his shoe, gravity tipped his hat to reveal a lifelike stink finger tattoo festooned prominently on the top of his head. I asked why. He said, "I've been having chemo right now and if anybody stares, I tip my hat to them."

Roger Barton is a musician and teacher terminally living in Frankfort, Illinois; lastly, verbal concision is not his forte, but he is up to the challenge.

Sarah's Hands

Sarah woke up without her hands. They were gone—severed clean with a surgical instrument. No trace left behind, just a pool of blood seeping through the sheets. Don't panic, she told herself. Stop the bleeding and call for help. But she couldn't dial 9-1-1 without her hands.

Francis DiClemente is a writer and video producer who lives in Syracuse, New York. *francisdiclemente.com*

The Old Dog

His uncle left everything to charity, and he inherited the cantankerous dog. It was old, with a weeping eye. He paid the vet's bills and gave it food but no love. They lived in mute, reproachful companionship until the dog died and the man mourned a life of failed relationships.

Madeleine McDonald has a go at many forms of writing. Facebook *@madeleinemcdonald*

Divided Loyalties

They were family friends. She'd welcomed her, pyjama'd, at 11:30 p.m., loved her daughter, cooked when she cried for Syria. Their move away was nothing, compared to the announcement that she would remain "neutral" in the face of a family split. For the victim of abuse, this felt like the ultimate betrayal.

Karen Jones can usually be found dreaming by the sea, seizing opportunities for adventures, and loving the journey, dead ends and all.

Keeping Time

Ira penciled work hours in a ledger. After his death, I studied the log, not mere marks of cash due, but life notes: a friend's twins drowning; his house burning; his daughter's birth. Ira's accounting mistakes erased were always changed, his life's stories always changing were never erased.

Jack Albert is a poet, student of history, writer of small, ordinary, but important things.

Snapshot

Traditional furniture ready to be trucked away. Clothes bagged. Shoes sorted. Dishes, glassware, cutlery, knickknacks, playing cards, photographs boxed. Books, hardcovered and soft, CDs and DVDs laid out on the floor like a yard sale in progress. Yellowed package of cigarettes buried in a drawer. A snapshot of a life no longer.

Philip Goldberg's passion is fiction, from micro to short stories, many of which have been published.

Sometimes Dogs

I love them. With all of my heart, and I think they have hearts larger than we can fathom. But sometimes an itch, an irk, a buzzard gets trapped in their sweetness. The wolf inside stirs, and they lunge. Teeth everywhere. I forgive nature.

Elaina will always love dogs, as terrifying as it was ... *elainawrites.com*

Petty Theft

Confession: When you were waiting in the supermarket checkout line, little me snuck the coin stolen from Grandma's bingo jar behind my back and turned the job until the forbidden candy landed in my hungry palm. One time, the candy scattered to the ground. You believed my lie.

A special education teacher by day, Theresa Milstein writes middle grade, YA, and dabbles in poetry.

The Kitchen Waits

Food groups gargle as fruits (apples/pears) and vegetables (carrots/peppers) barter. Carbonated cola ruminates. Square pans and rectangular trays create lessons in crust and geometry. Chicken tenders bake. Dessert is to desert as kittens are to kites. Sticky quotes and alto notes stack. Traffic stalls for miles. Kitchen waits.

Jen Schneider is an educator who lives, works, and writes in small spaces throughout Pennsylvania.

Dead Heat

The rising cost of heating his home made him shiver. Thin blankets feebly fought off the cold until pneumonia wrapped itself around his lungs. Now, at the crematorium, he'll soon be warm. Next month, his only grandson will jet off to the sunshine of the Caribbean, burning through his inheritance.

John Holmes is a cyclist of short distances and a writer of short stories.

The Perfect Ad

Picture an indoor pool at a gym. Older women of a certain age, in various stages of fitness, enter the pool. Class begins. Bodies bob and move. The water begins to bubble and boil. Faces turn pink and pinker. A woman's voice: "Ladies, menopause heating you up? Try ..."

Bish Denham grew up in the US Virgin Islands and is the author of three children's books and numerous articles. Facebook *@bishdenham.author*

Night Jogging

As active as I was in the day, so I was in the night. I jumped into an active deep sleep, where my flailings woke my partner, but never me. Known sounds of traffic and airplanes were common and not a threat ... I woke refreshed.

Heather Hawk is a writer and gardener living a chaotic life. *heatherhawk.net*

Edmond Halley

She had met him at fourteen. He came to her from splintered darkness, out of a sea of lonely stars. Now at eighty-nine, she waits for his return. Praying he'll find her again using the secret co-ordinates to her heart—and that their love hadn't been doomed from the start.

Jass Aujla plans perfect (fictional) murders in between her day-job meetings. *jassaujla.com*

Christmas Eve

Christmas decorations jingle, as everybody scurries around her. Outside the snow is starting to settle. Meanwhile, she sits in the corner with her collection of bedtime stories for children. Rapunzel is letting down her golden locks, the town musicians of Bremen are playing. Alone, she is not lonely anymore.

Anika K. Clausen writes poems and short stories that entertain the dark corners of the mind while alluding to the masked realities of today. LinkedIn *@anika-kamilla-clausen*

The Land of Make Believe

When she was younger, she allowed herself to visit the land of Make Believe where she met some very nice people. All too soon, though, she was forced to return home to reality. She couldn't visit Make Believe again for at least six months—something to do with her temporary resident status, she was told.

Phillip Temples, of Watertown, Massachusetts, has published five mystery-thriller novels, a novella, and two short story anthologies in addition to over 190 short stories online. *temples.com*

Disillusioned

I wasn't the first to fall completely under his spell. Mesmerized, I believed him when he said he was an alchemist. But as soon as the smoke cleared and charm wore off, I saw that all he could conjure was meth of poor quality … and a leaden trail of broken hearts.

Jessica Needle is a naturopathic doctor who every so often pulls off a nifty magic trick of her own.

Victory for a 9th-grade "Bitch"

Every morning they stood there, a perfect circle of name-brand, superficial fluff. I stood there, smoking, ignoring their laughter, their "bitch" taunts directed at me. A deep drag filled me with courage. I squeezed between their shoulders and exhaled. Choking smoke silenced their laughter, distorted their perfect circle.

Mary Schreiner lives in Green Bay, Wisconsin. She enjoys pine forests and the way corn fields wither in fall. Facebook *@maryschreiner*

Promise

On the gibbous promise of brighter futures in greener pastures, we imagined neon gardens, compared to which, green bills buying marble mansions, look dull. The neon signs say we'll get there, like an A, an alphabet that means so much and so little. Not unlike neon gardens promised in afterlife.

Dr.Vaishnavi Pusapati is a physician and a writer, published/forthcoming in *The Drabble, Plum Tree Tavern, Dreich Magazine* and *Paragraph Planet.*

In Memory of Things to Come

Dad sups his porridge as I pop pills from blister packs into his dose-a-day dispenser. It must be Thursday then. The routine has ticked away his life, and mine. But our time is done. Now a care home nurse will measure out our weeks and months and years—on Thursdays.

Avery Mathers keeps bees in the Scottish Highlands, but mostly he writes.

Enough is Enough

It started, with hopes, dreams, and excitement, on November 25. Thirty-nine years later, it ended, the denouement a hearing, on the 24th. That synchronicity pleased her, as did the fact it wasn't forty years. She left the court liberated, free, giving the gold symbol of her imprisonment to a beggar.

Karen Jones can usually be found dreaming by the sea, seizing opportunities for adventures and loving the journey, dead ends and all.

Weightless

I am thinking cosmic thoughts when a cobweb comes into view. Bam! Invisible in most lights, waving softly on a late summer morning, it grounds me with an unfathomable weight. "Come back to earth. Clean your house." I ignore it (I have for months, maybe?) and return to the stars.

Deborah Jones wanted to be a tugboat captain but, with some regret, chose broadcast news writing instead.

Dissidence

Loud male voices sustain a bassy backdrop for female twang. The song could be country, but it's simply the soundtrack to country living.

Jessica Bell hates country music, and clearly country living too.

Driving

It's been a long drive. Three days on the road and now, almost home. The landscape has assumed a familiar, comforting air. "Turnpike back or backroads?" "Whatever." "It's a nice day, backroads." Four hours, 150 miles, six driveways. We're in bloody nowhere. Mr. "I Don't Like GPS" missed the turn.

Barbara Elliott is a Philadelphia-based artist, writer, and lover of baseball.

Vanishing

A cloudless sky, rain soft as skin. This is how I bury you, at the edge of the old aquifer, tangled in snowdrops and honeysuckle. You will be safe here, honey, no one will look for you, no one will know what you have done.

Lorette C. Luzajic writes, publishes, edits, and teaches flash fiction. She is also an internationally collected visual artist. *mixedupmedia.ca*

Wrinkles of Disappointment

Each remembered mortification etches grooves in her cheeks. On the right: Oxfords when she'd asked for Mary Janes; miscarriage; promotions awarded to rivals. The left: Misspelling "woebegone" in the championship bee; her husband's affairs, discovered posthumously; being swaddled in adult diapers. One memory reveals two dimples nestled within the folds.

At five feet give or take, author Ann S. Epstein appreciates "short" but also favors "long" earrings, slumbers, and summer evenings. *asewovenwords.com*

Dementia Prayer

The kind-eyed dementia therapist smiled; she reassured me as I struggled to pass that assessment, to repeat those words: "Hand ..." "park ..." "nylon ..." "yellow ..." "carrot ..." The first word echoed, the others floated away as I silently prayed that she would hold my hand, speak different words, and magically make everything better.

Mary Schreiner lives in Green Bay, WI where she enjoys pine forests and the way corn fields wither in fall. Facebook *@maryschreiner*

Sorrow

On his tired hands, abandoned on the gray boards of his worktable, heavy, hot and bitter tears flowed. He cried the first time in his life ... with grief, with real tears. He was crying for the loss of his dog Rex, whom he had just buried in the garden.

Nicolae Dumitru is a retired mechanical diplomat and an engineer and writer from Constanta City, Romania.

Gnawing

I gnaw on the bones of trauma to get the last gristle most people would avoid. Use all my strength to crack femurs, suck in the marrow. I dump the carcass and organs into a cast iron pot to transform it all into life-sustaining broth. You never understood my process.

A special education teacher by day, Theresa Milstein writes middle grade, YA, and dabbles in poetry. *theresamilstein.blogspot.com*

Cousins

The cousins look nothing alike: the son curled in a ball, fists clenched, wide-eyeing his rival on their grandparents' bed; the nephew stretched the full length of his twenty-four inches, arms outstretched, like Jesus. Twenty-five years later, the cousins break bread and drink wine at the family table.

Becky Jo Gesteland lives in Ogden, Utah, where she teaches English-related subjects and writes flash prose. *jomamabecky.org*

Estate Sale

Another move another purge. At seventy, she knows this may be her last. The sorting is weightier this time. Whatever she keeps, one day, someone else will sort, separate the wheat of her life from chaff. If there is to be a Last Judgement, that's who will make it.

Jonathan Odell has published three novels and lives with his husband in Minneapolis, Minnesota. *jonathanodell.com*

Water to a Whale

The environment. Everything around us, within us. Water to a whale. Air to an albatross. Earth to an earwig. So essential yet so not seen. Like dripping water torture, we alter it; slowly consume it. It has no voice. Its only response is to deprive us of life as we sleepwalk.

Chris Lihou is a retired and trying to find deeper understanding via writing; mostly poetry.

Coal Poaching

Living on a mining town's windy ridge, Junior poached coal fallen from hopper's rolling through the valley. His colliery collection, cheaper, more safely mined than from bituminous pits below, forge-warmed his winter nights. Black gold dross, stove ashes, scuttle spread on springtime seedlings, nurturing summer's garden, encouraged fall's early harvest.

Jack Albert is a poet, student of history, writer of small, ordinary, but important things.

Triangulated

The Greek figure Isosceles thought he was well-balanced, seeing himself as a stable genius. But he had a reputation for squaring off with people and being pointy-headed. He pushed these characterizations aside, hired himself a new hair stylist, and boasted that, regardless, he'd always find undying support from his base.

Joel Savishinsky's collection *Our Aching Bones, Our Breaking Hearts: Poems on Aging,* will be out in 2023. *ithaca.edu/savishin*

Change

Never able to cope with change, he's now desperate for it. Six different schools, three fathers, and eight homes dismantled him; leaving him to pick up his own pieces. Loose relationships and unsecured employment weakened him further. He shakes his cracked cup at a passer-by. "Spare me change," he begs.

John Holmes is a cyclist of short distances and a writer of short stories.

Aging

I've never been this age before. How do I behave? Should I speak wise words of wisdom? Be calm and reassuring? Tell stories to children? Shit. Maybe I'll do an Eloise and pour a pitcher of water down the mail chute. But who remembers Eloise?

Bish Denham grew up in the US Virgin Islands and is the author of three children's books and numerous articles. Facebook *@bishdenham*

The

I love the alphabet. When my parents read to me as a child, the earliest word I recognized was "the." It floated serenely amid a sea of angular and rounded shapes. A profound discovery. I was happy whenever and wherever I found my new word-friend. I fell in love.

Susan Black is an artist and a writer who lives in Aurora, Oegon. *blackstarstudio.me*

The Warmth of Love

I stoke the fire in the wood stove to temper the morning chill. Steeped in loneliness, I take refuge in the treasured memories of you. On the wall, hangs your radiant portrait. My heart is comforted. The warmth of your smile manifests a spiritual love that dispels the morning chill.

Jay Hernandez loves to read and occasionally pen a short story.

Personas Non Grata

They're there, I note, scrubbing my hand down my face while looking in the mirror. They're always there. I sit down glumly, wondering, does anyone else see them when looking at me. Free time, I'm told. Come on, I tell the specters of my victims as I leave my cell.

Holly Keichel is a chocoholic polymathic square peg just trying to fit into the round hole of life.

On Nectar Queries and Cycles of Life

A hummingbird drinks nectar from a saucer as my daughter approaches with her palm cupped. A fly rests belly-up in the middle of her paint-stained hand. "What's wrong with him," she asks, eyes wide. My feet remain grounded—firmly planted in my soil-less kitchen. No sugar-coating. Nowhere to hide.

Jen Schneider is an educator who lives, works, and writes in small spaces throughout Pennsylvania.

Self-Portrait

Stranded on an island, I yearn without hope for rescue. Someone was here before. Their bones are left behind with a few personal belongings. I dare not touch them. Yet I use sand and my blood to draw my facial likeness in the sand. Might I be rescued today?

Heather Hawk is a writer and gardener living a chaotic life. *heatherhawk.net*

Little Pleasures

As the storm seethed, the lightning fulminated violently through the ghostly streets of their neighborhood. She was on edge about the whole idea. "It must be done," her husband snapped. "We need to bury him before tomorrow's auction." Forty years under her belt and Jenna still enjoys author's reading events.

Andrea Damic (Sydney, Australia) is an amateur photographer and author of micro fiction, flash fiction and poetry who usually writes at night, when everyone is asleep. *linktr.ee/damicandrea*

Touch

Bruce looks forward to the days that the aged care agency send their revolving door of shower people, not because he ever feels particularly unclean (he is obsessive with his wiping) but because it's the only time anyone gently touches his skin since his wife went to heaven without him.

Doug Jacquier is a keen vegetable gardener and cook and an occasional stand-up comedian, as well as doing the best he can as husband, father, grandfather, and great-grandfather. *sixcrookedhighwaysblog.wordpress.com*

I Remember

Christmas Eves of makeup and girlish laughter, returning barefooted, inebriated, and blissfully happy. Christmas Eves filling stockings, preparing the spectacle for expectant, shiny-eyed children, magic in the air. Christmas Eves of Midnight Mass, sopranos petitioning heaven with joyful carols. And this one. Beautiful for being transitional. Pain is cathartic.

Karen Jones can usually be found dreaming by the sea, seizing opportunities for adventures and loving the journey, dead ends and all.

Just Wanna

It was 1983, and "Girls Just Want to Have Fun" blared from the radio as she groomed the horse after her third lesson. She was having fun learning to walk, canter, and trot. But she didn't like galloping. At age thirteen, she wasn't ready for that much fun yet.

A special education teacher by day, Theresa Milstein writes middle grade, YA, and dabbles in poetry. *theresamilstein.blogspot.com*

Dirty Pictures

Behind the bushes along the garage, he shows it to her, dirt and dead bugs smeared across sticky pages that smell of piss. He points at a picture of a naked girl on her knees in front of something wet and torn away. "Wanna do that?" he asks the child.

Diane lives in the southwest US and has been doing nothing with her writing for a long time.

How Does Superman Fly?

Consumed in conversation, demonstrating their viewpoints, arms extended over the condiment bottles on the table. "No! Superman's hands were angled. Nope, they were extended straight. Sorry, tilted downward." Abruptly, the waitress yells, "Hey ya'll, we don't pray over ketchup here, knock it off!" Snickering, they scarfed their crab cakes.

Deb Obermanns is a traveler, lover of storytelling, and international schoolteacher.

Watching the Darkness

Diamonds sparkle through the cold night air. Okay, electric lights twinkle. Pick your illusion and defend it. Nearby, a police car pulls a vehicle over. An RV also stops. Inside the parking lot, I don't expect trouble, but you never know what lurks around a desert casino. Nothing is likely to happen, but anything could. I wait.

B. Lynn Goodwin is the owner of Writer Advice, and the author of a YA, a memoir, and a self-help book. *writeradvice.com*

Said Unsaid

The Mothers' Club gathers weekly at a member's home. They sit sipping wine or drinking coffee. While their very young children babble and shriek in the background, they talk in the foreground, going on about their kids and their husbands, laughing occasionally. But they never utter a word about themselves.

Philip Goldberg's passion is fiction, from micros to short stories, even a novel, many of which have been published.

Eve

There. There it is. That indescribable feeling so hard to describe. A quickening of the heartbeat, the small intake of breath, the fluttering in the stomach, the growing warmth in the groin whenever she sees the forbidden fruit ... Is it love or lust? She tosses the dice.

Bish Denham grew up in the US Virgin Islands and is the author of three children's books and numerous articles. Facebook *@bishdenham*

Surrounded

Due to a messy drawn-out battle in the settlement of the estate, the old barn now sits in the new subdivision, surrounded by McMansions. It's creating an opposite image of the gap due to a lost front tooth that is surrounded by an otherwise perfect line of white teeth.

Roy Dorman enjoys reading and writing speculative fiction and poetry.

Knife-Nicker Norman

Nowhere near No-man's-land, a Knife-Nicker named Norman knew no notoriety. Norman nicked knives nearly nightly notwithstanding the narrative. Nobody knew Norman's knife-nicking needs. Nightfall, Norman never negotiated necessary knickknacks to nick knives neatly. Nobody nudged the knife, knocking Norman. Knife-Nicker Norman nicked knives nevermore.

Anika K. Clausen writes poems and short stories that entertain the dark corners of the mind while alluding to the masked realities of today. LinkedIn *@anika-kamilla-clausen*

The Anniversary

The waiter filled two flutes. "Forty years!" she exclaimed. Two houses, three kids, four grands and here they were, recreating that long ago Maui honeymoon. He raised his glass, "To you." "To us!" She laughed. He struggled to recall the exact moment that laugh had transformed from endearing to annoying.

Barbara Elliott is a Philadelphia-based artist, writer, and lover of baseball.

Futonesque

She messaged, "We have a nice, spare futon." Futons had not occurred to me. Anyhow, it turned out the futon was too large. But. "I have another, smaller, newer, and your settee would love my space." Her insistent voice insisted. The inhabitant of a fraught life had arranged it all!

Jenny Dunbar is a writer and potter based in the UK.

Paris

It was Paris. It was spring. In a cafe. They were young. They were lonely. So they married. She was bored. He was bad. They stayed together. Then she died. It was Paris. It was winter. In a cafe. He was old. He was lonely. Her ghost came. His heart broke. Then—he died.

Paul Negri is a retired publisher, New York transplant to North Carolina, now happily writing fiction every day.

Karma

He poked. The puppy whined. "Stop that!" Old Lady Sims! His buddies ran. He was on his knees. "Seeing if it's dead." She pushed him backwards. "Bully AND a liar. You know karma? Someday it'll be *you* under the stick." She scooped up the puppy and turned. Mean old hag.

Michaele Jordan (who says she's a bit odd) was born in LA, educated in New York, and lives in Cincinnati, and she's worked at a kennel, a Hebrew School, and AT&T.

On Long Routes Home

At home in the seventies-era kitchen, the AI-powered world waits. I hope to make it there by nightfall. Traffic spirals, the transmission sputters, and the Honda hesitates. A gull squawks. Souls in rubber soles press gas pedals, both manufactured and fractured. What forms of waiting do we most anticipate?

Jen Schneider is an educator who lives, works, and writes in small spaces throughout Pennsylvania.

Fear

Dana, a motorman, took miners to pit and back, scuttling coal, seam to tipple scale in between. Electrified, his clattering machine sped arc-flashed in anthracite darkness. Men feared for their lives his reckless speed, only coal should come from the mine broken and crushed.

Jack Albert is poet, student of history, and writer of small things.

The Devil's In The Details

Jason looked forward to his date with Jane who he had found on Lovematch, a dating site. He expected, as with all of his other dates, she would fall in love with him. However, when they met, Jane told him "I'm collecting your soul. Your agreement with Satan has expired."

The author (Doug Hawley) is a little old man who lives with Sharon and cat Kitzhaber. *google.com/site/aberrantword*

Betrayal

Crying softly to herself, dressed in her gladrags, mascara leaving streaks on her cheeks, she looks in the mirror, to fix her face, and herself, temporarily, at least. Her birthday party awaits. She was not expecting to discover her husband's secret family, on this of all days. Stiff upper lip ...

Karen Jones can usually be found dreaming by the sea, seizing opportunities for adventures and loving the journey, dead ends and all.

The Hunter

The hunter cut into the leathery flesh of the monster. Disposing of monsters was arduous work, but thoughts filled with family reinforced his will. Unsettling roars came from the obsidian blackness beyond. The monster's companions. The hunter readied his sword with a strained, but confident gruff. The hunt begins again.

Patrick Cavallone is an aspiring writer with a love of horror and fantasy!

Bunny and Bear

"I will sunder you in half." A circular saw whirred to life, the conveyor belt inching forward. Bunny fought against his restraints, but it was no use. The blade crept closer. "Noah, dinner!" The boy looked at the stuffed rabbit. "Sorry, Bunny. I'll have Mr. Bear save you after dinner."

Shea Ballard is a fantasy writer who lives in the Phoenix area. *sheaballard.com*

Democracy

Some feared unfamiliarity: hated it as vile. Bigotry in myriad forms stained their souls. Others embraced diversity and celebrated differences. None were perfect. All worshiped at the same shrine. When evil forces threatened their Goddess, they rose like valiant warriors. United, they cupped Democracy in their hands, and saved her.

Tony Tinsley is a professor emeritus of psychology and an author and editor who divides his time between the Pacific Northwest and the heartland in the United States.

Pine

A barren pine with skeletal branches towers above my window. Once it thrived. Now its cones hold fast to its decaying frame. We both sway with the wind, not sure of when it will snap us. Lightning flashed, lit the view as the barren pine cracked and ripped in two.

Jessica Binkley is a novelist, academic support tutor, and MFA grad based in the southeast. *jessicabinkley.com*

The Dying Flaneur

I stroll past stores and cafes and bars and clubs that are no longer there. I catch no one's eye on this street. Memories dissipate behind me in the wake of my ambling. Incessant are the blaring horns of city traffic as I sink deeper and deeper into insignificance.

Gary McElroy, after forty-five years in NYC, is still trying to fit in. Anywhere.

Cheers

She insisted we had fizz. And who were we to argue? Who wants the cork? Jack shouted, it's meant to bring good luck! Hmmm, I thought, I could do with some luck but yet, here we were, guests at Bubbles' funeral, drinking her champagne. I gave the cork a miss.

Ellen Fox is an award-winning playwright, who has also written for radio, film, and television.

Whiskey Rebellion

"Charity, you gotta take this world by the balls!" her father blared on nights whiskey was his date. She'd nod, wait until he was asleep, set his glass on the table, then head to bed, knowing the only thing she'd grab was the first chance to get out of town.

Suzanne Miller is the author of *Queen* and *Temperatures*. *tattooeddaughter.wordpress.com*

Social Problems

Stephanie chronicles every aspect of her life on social media. She even details her family's long list of illnesses. She posts recipe videos. She makes documentaries of every road trip. None of my business. But I can't believe she's on a cruise again. Can I both envy and despise her?

Gip Plaster has always been compelled to write, so he does: first journalism, now website content and microfiction. *17wordstories.com*

On Being Late

The road was black as the night. The wet surface shimmering with the oncoming headlights. He sped on. Being late was simply not an option. The deer came out of nowhere. Braking, spinning he now faced the vehicle that was behind. He stood no chance. He was never late again.

Chris Lihou is retired and trying to find deeper understanding via writing; mostly poetry.

Twenty Second Subway Romance

I stand in the aisle on a crowded express. You sit facing me. I don't know where to look, but soon find my eyes drifting over you. Your glimpse catches mine and I like what I see. You don't turn away, right away. No words exchanged in our twenty-second romance.

Ken Romanowski is a semi-retired financial professional, adjunct instructor, history buff, and storyteller. Facebook *@kenromanowski*

Harsh Wind

I stand drenched in sunlight. Ominous ink-dark clouded sky ahead. A harsh winter wind hurls autumn-dead leaves and detritus without remorse. Dogs cower, frighted by the screaming air. I push onward. Storm's a-comin'. A disembodied voice crackles through the tempest: "Welcome to Starbuck's, may I take your order?"

Streeper Clyne feels blessed to live a creative life; crafting worlds and imagery with words.

Figment

"There's nothing to tell," she says with a devilish voice. "I'm here, aren't I." "If only you were," I say to the shadow—wishing. Then I hear her again. Soft, laughing. The shadow starts to dance and whispers, "I miss you too, but I had no choice." And she's gone.

Pasquale Trozzolo is a retired madman from Kansas, and his work gets around. *pasqualetrozzolo.com*

The Escape

Suicidal thoughts stream in on the morning light. Unwanted and intrusive, they try to break my spirit. "You can't fix this, they say, "End your life, escape the pain." "These distressing thoughts are normal," my therapist assures me. "I've had them myself." I'm still suicidal, but not today. I hope.

Patricia Pollack loves traveling then coming home to a city life in Philadelphia, Pennsylvania.

After the Storm

KYW warns of fog and broken taillights as metal forks kiss plastic spoons. Chicken tenders and beef barley soup banter with corn-flakes and frosted wheat squares. The children eat. Winds hiss at window cracks. Kettles whistle, then puff. Through the foggy mist, I see a rainbow. The sun rises.

Jen Schneider is an educator who lives, works, and writes in small spaces throughout Pennsylvania.

Raclette for the Holidays

The ideal dinner, a plethora of food complemented with a wealth of wine. The euphoric evening effortlessly progresses; guests entertained by witty conversation until "fake news" rears up, leaving the hostess with limited options. Acknowledge reality or vamoose, "and remember to take your sour grapes", as the door slams.

Deb Obermanns is an avid traveler, lover of storytelling, and international schoolteacher.

Motherlove

My mother's hug was usually an excuse to frisk my midriff. "How can you go around half-naked?"—noting the absence of a camisole. Young people run hot, I reasoned. Now, I pull one out when it hits fifty-nine degrees or lower. The stretchy fabric is a caress without the scold.

Deborah Jones, a former broadcast journalist, wonders if she'll recognize intelligent life on Earth if she should stumble across it.

Composition in Blue

I've learned from Mondrian to organize my world into separate mental sectors—chores, time with friends, time to read and rest. However, one small square's reserved, painted the infinite blue of a wild open sky where I can retreat from the mundane to my imagination, emotion, dreams.

Joan Leotta plays with words on page and stage under the blue skies of North Carolina as well as in the blue spaces in her own mind. *mainstreetragbookstore.com*

Way Off Course

No one told my American Eskimo dog the Iditarod isn't run in the desert. She drags me through dirt and sagebrush, a far cry from Alaska, like I'm a dog sled musher except she doesn't heed my commands, but we pretend we're sledding anyway and who cares if we win?

Marc Littman just adopted a white American Eskimo rescue dog who sheds like a blizzard and loves dragging him out for long walks in the chill of night.

Authenticity

Having worn masks forever, possible ways to live her life felt like a shopping list. She took different lives, and tried them on, like hats: bold, colorful, classy, frivolous. Potentially, she looked good in all of them: they worked. But she decided that accessories weren't necessary. She was enough.

Karen Jones can usually be found dreaming by the sea, seizing opportunities for adventures and loving the journey, dead ends and all.

The Other Son

On a sunny day when she thinks she should be happy, she pushes her baby son in a swing that looks like a bucket supporting him safely. Amidst her son's giggles, she mourns the twin she could not keep safe, the one who did not survive his birth.

Fran Abrams is a Maryland poet who enjoys writing regardless of the form. *franabramspoetry.com*

So Much Alike

This morning, I am my mother—brisk, critical, full of cheerleader energy. The sun brims, strong morning coffee I drink black, birds not awake yet. I listen for the veery's notes to rise, the way bubbles rise in the percolator dome, long-gone Mother's bright red lipstick on my cup's rim.

Dale Champlin writes short stories in long hand—this story could have been a lot longer!

"T"

No towns, only deeply-shaded side roads wandering from the serpentine two-lane highway. Sky clearing, the sunlight sharp and crisp on the pavement, curving among the trees. At ridge top, views of the city. On the horizon, the Bay sparkled. A "T" in the road. "which way?"

"Any way but back."

J. Frank Papovich writes about mountains, motorcycles, and the American West.
mtsmotorswest.blog

Supper

Age four, my favorite chicken, Old One-Eye, was gone. I asked, Don't you miss him? The others cackled and beaked. Great Aunt Bert chuckled, said she'd wrung his neck for our supper. And hadn't he tasted good? Profound shame in knowing chicken meant those warm beings and food in my belly.

Janet is a SF Bay Area writer, editor, teacher. *janettecwolf.net*

Conclusion

She leaned forward to signal caring, "What I want to leave you with today is this: first and last, be true ..." All those adolescent faces like butter left too long on the kitchen counter. Today bland, tomorrow rancid. "And that's it," she said, for once grateful they'd have no questions.

Miriam N. Kotzin writes both fiction and poetry, and her most recent novel is *Right This Way* from Spuyten Duyvil Press.

Dips and Lips

When she smiles, dimples form. Her jeweled necklace complements her plunging neckline. At a lull in the music, I ask, “Care to dance?” I dance my practiced moves. Holding her close, she leans back and extends her arm overhead. Bending to plant my first kiss, she slips through my hands.

Charles Gray lives in Texas with his wife and enjoys playing chess and writing flash fiction.

Midnight Snack

Torn to bits during the night like a casualty of war, my ripe, red tomatoes were left bleeding in the dirt, their remains swarmed by flies and oozing maggots. The morning sun cast no shadow on the crumpled wire fence, folded over itself and stomped flat during the senseless invasion.

Rita Riebel Mitchell writes in southern New Jersey, where she lives amongst the trees and wildlife with her husband. *ritariebelmitchell.com*

How Will I Know?

Dancing class for gym credit was run by the impossibly fit teacher with frosted hair and talons who also ran the school's halftime show. This class was beneath her. She said to do "The Madonna" move. Students turned left. I turned right. Whitney Houston made it look effortless.

A special education teacher by day, Theresa Milstein writes middle grade, YA, and dabbles in poetry. *theresamilstein.blogspot.com*

Unwanted Lover

Leering. Arms open wide. Beckoning to her. Calling her name. But she rebuffs. Turns her back. Steps farther away. Slams the door. Closes the blinds. Hides alone. Finally, after months, ventures out only to feel long fingers grasp her throat, her chest, her head. The red line appears. It's COVID.

Teri M Brown, author of *An Enemy Like Me*, connects readers with characters they'd love to invite to lunch. *terimbrown.com*

The Portal

Standing at the boarding gate; luggage filled with misplaced anxieties, depressions; loneliness—COVID leftovers. The passenger boarding bridge is my gateway between one world and the next. The alloy cylinder, my portal to freedom, teleports me from source to destination. Hope is now a path to a wondrous new world.

Ilona Rapin is addicted to the curiosity and excitement of wandering the world which inspires her to write short stories about her impressions.

Love is a Habit

I woke up, the bed unfamiliarly cold. The kettle whistled louder this morning. I drank one more cup of coffee than I usually do and ate a second serving of eggs. I flipped the newspaper to the sports section and handed the crossword puzzle to her.

Andrew Inocencio is a United States Air Force veteran working on a collection of short stories and poetry. Instagram *@inocencio.andrew*

Dolly

She loved everything about Dolly Parton. Her voice. Her boobs. Her blonde hair. Just everything. And, though she'd only seen Dolly on TV, she knew if they ever met—like at the Dollywood amusement park—they'd prove to be fast friends. If only Momma hadn't loved Dolly, too, Jolene mused.

Keith Hoerner (BS, MFA) is founding editor of the Webby-Award-recognized *Dribble Drabble Review,* an online literary ezine and print anthology series of all things "little-ature."

A Quiet Seethe

He won't care if it's lamb or pork. Nothing she offers compares with the stock market, which changes more often than her days. She puts plates on the table then calls her mother from the kitchen. Better a recap of Guy Lombardo than the ticker tape in her husband's eyes.

Janey Skinner writes, draws, and blunders in Richmond, California. *writer.janeyskinner.com*

Bird Lady

It wasn't a regular morning. Her hunched form behind net curtains, rhythmically swaying with knife in hand. She uttered a slow whine as she deftly cut and shaped each morsel. The bird tables were empty, various paraphernalia, used to entice and procure, strung in pathetic lines. Garden fancies intermittently blinking.

Jenny writes and makes abstract ceramics.

Interview with the Depressed Vampire

The Count, sick of the coffin and the cape and all those pale beautiful necks with throbbing veins, opened the drapes and stepped onto the deck to view his first sunrise in centuries. Who needs a wooden stake when the bright lights of morning can burn you into oblivion, into dust?

Chuck Augello has a new book coming out about Kurt Vonnegut. *cdawriting.com*

Root Canal

The X-ray flooded the screen in shades of gray. You, with your smiling eyes and pristine scrubs, explained the procedure efficaciously. There are reasons, I thought, why dentistry only admits movie stars. Unsettled, I imagined tiny boats sailing down my tooth's root. Unconvinced, I took my referral and ran.

Mel is a British stay-at-home mom living in Maryland who enjoys writing way more than going to the dentist. Instagram *@meledden*

The Line of Time

I got the years wrong again. I only figured it out because I was remembering something else, trying to fix its point in time. Otherwise, the timeline wouldn't make sense. Memories are like a spine's articulations, one anchoring another, and time is the skeleton of the body we live in.

Amy Goldmacher is an anthropologist, a writer, and a book coach. She can be found at *amygoldmacher.com*

A Cheese Dream

I had not been in bed very long. When four balloon men came along. One was red and one was blue, yellow were the other two. First they danced around my bed, Then they bounced upon my head. My morning alarm call was such a relief.

Peter Snell was a bookseller and he wears a lot of red in December. Facebook *@bartonsbookshop*

Options

I went out for a walk as the only trick left. While wandering around, I heard a couple of strangers—You have two options, survive or ... I couldn't hear anymore. I decided that this was a divine sign, fate wasn't offering me any other option. Survival was my only alternative.

Veronica (aka Vero Rumor) is a Spaniard living in Brighton, UK, who writes poetry and takes photos to understand the world (and herself). *veroruiz.home.blog*

Metempsychosis

I fly, like an undisciplined kite, aimless, with kaleidoscope vision of multiple others I cannot discern well. I soar, I plummet, I soar. Weightless, untethered to concerns, misgivings or unconfessed sins. Soaring, plummeting, a vague memory of floating to the ground. So brief. A mayfly? That fleeting? That insignificant?

Gary McElroy is still in NYC, wheels spinning, killing time whittling pieces from earlier writings.

Balance

We follow the crowd out of the conference room. Which session you going to next? The one on meditation. I need to balance my chakras. Oh yeah. I check the itinerary. You coming? *Nah. I don't like breathing.* She turns to look at me. I shrug. *It makes me dizzy.*

L. J. Caporusso reluctantly has a blog on *ljcaporusso.com*—it's all right. (It's weird.)

The Science of Parking

Your parking routine upon arriving home is immutable: Lean out of your car window and align the wheels with that spot on the curb. Forward and back, forward and back. You shake your head and drive off, looping around the neighborhood for another attempt. Forward and back . . .

Streeper Clyne lives on a quiet street among colorful neighbors, aware that she adds to the mélange.

The Bolt

A strange sense of the inevitable came to him. Hair bristled on his arms. Passersby turned curious faces towards him. The woods held oddly silent. Then he looked from the clearing and saw lightning strike the white cliff. The bolt proved everything he'd felt. Even the thunder couldn't help agreeing.

Norbert Kovacs lives and writes in Hartford, Connecticut. *norbertkovacs.net*

First Quit

Evie stumbles reason to reason to reason. Bad pay, worse hours, how it is grim and endless and she is made invisible. She stands on the unyielding totality; she stomps. The bottom breaks out and reveals a hatch. Evie drops in, hits ground, and strides away in the new light.

Evan Harris is the author of *The Quit. suspendedsurveystory.net*

Fetching

Without warning, Cyrus, my one-eyed feline co-conspirator, will demand a game of fetch. Unlike a Labrador, who will retrieve over and over ad nauseum, Cyrus will stop abruptly. When he does, I'm reminded of the speed at which my ex-fiancé, [REDACTED], decided she fell out of love with me.

S. Barron Thompson resides in New Jersey and is the first in his family to both graduate college and live in a trailer park where he has found the greatest sense of community he's ever experienced.

The Bequest

My granddaughter reaches under my sweater, grabs a handful of soft belly—snorts her deep belly laugh. Is this where my mother came from? She gives me a sideways glance—knows I won't be here forever. Will you give me your unicorn earrings when ... when I get my ears pierced?

Dale Champlin writes short stories in long hand—this story could have been a lot longer!

Dieting

Being on a calorie-counting, controlled diet to lose weight kept bearing fruit for my husband, but not for me. The weighing scale always seemed partial towards him. Frustrated and annoyed at seeing yet another dip on the scale, I called out, "That's brain matter lost, not body weight!"

Divya George is an occasional writer.

On the Triangularity of Time

A child sits crisscrossed applesauce on the kitchen floor and reads *A Wrinkle in Time*, the dogeared paperback's corner folded neatly on page ninety-nine. Word tracings are to whipped butter as laugh lines are to moments in suspension. Batter drops as wonderings meander. Skin and denim folds sag—limbs lock.

Jen Schneider is an educator who lives, writes, and works in small spaces throughout Pennsylvania.

As Is

I set up my yard sale table where he'd parked his Camry. Gifts: Three identical teddy bears. A kitten cream pitcher. Abandoned: Almost-full bottle Cuervo Gold. Pack of BICs. A soft blue flannel shirt I'd laundered until he wasn't there anymore. Helium-filled balloons swayed above my hand-lettered sign: ALMOST FREE!

Miriam N. Kotzin writes both fiction and poetry, and her most recent novel is *Right This Way*.

Printed in the USA
CPSIA information can be obtained
at www.ICGtesting.com
CBHW011713221023
1397CB00007B/6

9 783988 320360